"How dare you sa[...]
don't cook for you [...]

Angry tears sped down Carole's cheeks.

"I didn't say that." Daniel's tight-lipped retort was delivered slowly and deliberately. "I said you aren't showing your love for me the way you used to."

"That's not fair. I told you I had been up half the night with the baby."

"Nevertheless, it's a fairly accurate picture of the way things have been going around here lately." His voice took on a more conciliatory tone. "All I want is time for *us*, Carole. Time to love and laugh and share. The only thing we ever discuss is the baby." His hand reached for hers across the table. "I know Tim takes a lot of your time, but *I* need you, too."

Carole was stunned by his confession of loneliness. But she was also angry. "I should think a mature man would understand that this is only temporary. Tim won't be tiny forever. But right now I owe it to him to give him the best start I can. . . even if you feel I'm putting him first."

He faced her squarely. "I can see we have some tough times ahead of us if you don't learn how to mother Tim, not smother him. I love you, and I'll wait for you. But, remember, I'm only a man. Don't make me wait too long."

LINDA HERRING is the mother of four grown children and the wife of a Lutheran minister. Her writing is an avenue of ministry whereby she both entertains and uplifts with her down-to-earth view of Christianity.

Yesterday's Tomorrows

Linda Herring

Heartsong Presents

To Mel,
who championed this book
and to
Fay Palmer and Theresa Cotton
with my deepest thanks for their help.

ISBN 1-55748-440-6

YESTERDAY'S TOMORROWS

one

In the dim light of the hospital chapel, Daniel Thornton knelt to pray at the altar, bringing his petition like so many others. As a minister, he had been here before, to intercede for a desperately ill parishioner or to comfort a family in the freshness of their grief. Now the specter of death hovered over one of his own, and his faith was being put to the ultimate test.

He wanted to pray aloud, but his throat was tight with unshed tears. So he lifted his eyes to the small stained glass window and talked to his God silently.

Lord, our newborn son already belongs to you. Carole and I committed him to you even before his birth. You have so richly blessed the two of us with our love for one another, and now Timothy, the fruit of that love. Don't let him die. Please, God, don't take him from us.

Daniel let the tears slide down his well-formed cheeks and brushed back his curly brown hair with a careless hand. Feeling a measure of peace and strength return to his terribly tired body, he rose from his knees and prepared to visit his wife up on the maternity floor.

The door of the room glided open to reveal Carole sitting in the rocker by the window, holding their little son in her arms. Daniel stood for a moment to drink in the scene.

The traditional picture of mother and child was marred by the I.V. tube coming out of the baby's head, his tiny hands restrained at his sides by diaper pins fastened to the

5

sleeves of his gown.

Carole's dark auburn hair tumbled down around her shoulders, framing a pale face, and her smoky eyes were half closed as she rocked their child and hummed a simple melody. She nuzzled the top of his head close to the spot where the tube was inserted, and kissed the fine, dark hair.

"Hi," Daniel whispered.

"Hi." She lifted her head to receive his light kiss on her upturned mouth.

"How's the baby?" He touched Tim's little hand, and the fingers immediately curled around his finger. "There's not much strength in that grip. Yet he looks so perfect except for that I.V. in his head."

Carole gave her husband a weak smile. "He's a handsome lad, just like his father." She wanted to scream out, *Is he going to die? What happened? Surely God isn't going to take our baby!* Instead, she said in a throaty voice, "This isn't the way the books said it would be."

"No." Daniel knelt to give her an awkward hug, and Timothy released his father's finger and balled his hand into a soft fist. "But he's so beautiful, so perfectly formed. How can there be anything wrong with him?"

The door swung open with authority, and a nurse entered. "Time to take the baby to X-ray, Mrs. Thornton. You can carry him and I'll push his I.V. pole." She gave Daniel an inquisitive look as he unfolded his lanky frame and got to his feet.

"I'm coming, too," he announced, relieved when she nodded in agreement. Daniel was used to being in command of his world, but for the past two days hospital routine had largely ignored the respect to which he was accustomed. Here he was just another worried parent.

With Carole carrying the infant, the nurse rolling the intravenous equipment, and Daniel bringing up the rear, their little party drew a few interested stares from people in the hallways as they made their way to the lab.

The technician scratched his jaw in surprise when they arrived. "*Two days*? I thought this baby was two *months* old. Well, Mom, you'll have to help us a little. When I say go, I want you to pull the baby's arms up over his head. Here, put this shield around you."

Carole was shaking by the time the procedure was over, Timothy having screamed in protest of the indignities done to his miniature form. Meanwhile, Daniel had paced the hallway outside, hearing the distressed baby's cries, but helpless to rescue him.

Timothy was still snuffling against Carole's chest as they returned to their room. She laid him in the infant seat that had been positioned inside the baby bed and sank down into the nearby rocker.

"He sleeps in that?" Daniel asked.

"Yes. The doctors want him in an upright position so whatever liquid I can get down him stays there." Her face reflected her concern. "I can't understand why he can't keep anything down. He's not supposed to be moved at all. I'm not even supposed to hold him, really," she added guiltily, "but I know he needs the comfort. Besides," she admitted, glancing at Daniel miserably, "if he dies, I want to be able to remember how he felt . . . to—to be sure he knew his mother loved him very much." She stifled a sob and turned into her husband's arms for his strong embrace. When they parted she could see the stricken look on his face, the tears glistening in his eyes.

There was a soft knock on the door. It opened slowly to

admit Carol's best friend. Joyce Novelli came in, enfolding Carole in a sympathetic embrace. "We're praying for all of you. What can I do to help right now? Have you eaten?"

"Thank you for the prayers, and yes, I've eaten."

Joyce turned an inquiring look on her pastor. "What about you, Daniel? Is there anything I can do for you?"

"Your prayers are the most important thing." Daniel's smile was tired, but his voice was sincere as he added, "It's a wonderful thing to be ministered to by your congregation. Everyone has been so kind."

"We're only doing for you what you've done for us countless times," Joyce assured him. "And we love you both . . . or should I say, the three of you? Now can I see him?" She bent over the crib. "Ohh, he's beautiful. Hello, little Timothy. Do you know how blessed you are to have such a wonderful mother and father? You get well soon so we can show you off to the whole world." She leaned down and kissed his sleeping face, then gave a little shiver. "I wish they didn't have to put that tube in his head."

"That feeding tube is what's keeping him alive right now," Carole explained. "I try to think of it as another umbilical cord."

Joyce laughed softly. "Yeah, that sounds like something you would say." She cocked her head and regarded her friend fondly. "Your Irish is showing. For you, the glass is always half full. Between that and your faith, you're going to be fine." Her expression sobered. "But no matter what, I'm here for you. Just tell me what to do."

"Right now there is only one thing any of us can do," Daniel said. "Pray."

He was returning from walking Joyce to the elevator,

when a voice called out. "Pastor! Pastor Thornton!" Susan Lapney came scurrying up. An attractive woman in her thirties, Susan was one of the more erratic members of St. John's. "Pastor, how is the baby? I came just as soon as I heard the news."

"We don't know anything for sure, but he seems to be stable at the moment. It was nice of you to come down."

"It's just so sad. I wanted you to know I was thinking about you. And Carole, too, of course."

"Carole and the baby are down the hall." Daniel turned to lead the way.

But Susan stopped him. "Oh, I don't want to bother them. Just know that all of you are in my prayers." She flashed a brilliant smile. "I'll be back. If you need anything, please give me a call."

"Thank you, we will." Daniel was disappointed that Susan had declined his invitation to see his new son, but she was already stepping onto the elevator. She gave him a little wave as the door closed. "Strange lady," he mused, heading back toward the baby's room, "but I like her perfume."

The hospital routine was winding down for the night, the only sounds the swish of a nurse's soft-soled shoes in the corridor or an occasional page issued in a crisp monotone over the PA system. All the lights were out now except for the night light. Daniel stretched out on Carole's hospital bed. "A mite on the hard side, isn't it?"

"Doesn't matter. I don't think I'll get to use it much tonight anyway."

Daniel cradled his hands behind his head, while Carole put the baby in his little carrier and sat back down in the rocker.

"Do you know what today is?" he asked. When she shook her head, he went on. "It's the beginning of my tenth year here in Longview."

Carole sighed heavily. "This isn't much of a celebration, I'm afraid."

Daniel studied her profile in the half light. "Can't think of anywhere I'd rather be. I'm with *you*. Even if it's a sad time, we're together."

"I remember the first time I heard you preach," she reminisced. "I was so nervous about seeing you again. I didn't think you'd remember me."

"How could I forget the woman I was going to marry?" he teased, then his voice took on a reflective tone. "When Ellen died, I was sure I would never love again. And then one hot Sunday morning, there you were, looking lovelier than when I had last seen you. I have to confess, it came to me right away that your Samuel was dead, too. But what a chase you led me on! I've never had to work so hard to convince someone I loved them."

"Humph! I knew you loved me. I just had to be convinced to live in a parsonage again. Once burned, twice shy, you know." Her voice softened. "I'll have to admit, it's been mostly wonderful."

"Mostly?"

"Need I remind you of Mrs. Charles, Teletype Tillie, Polly and her suicide attempt at Thanksgiving, my running away to Galveston?"

"Okay, okay, so we've had our rough spots. What marriage hasn't? But—" he coached, waiting for her response.

"But I'm glad I married you anyway—" she replied

obediently. Her eyes flooded with tears as she looked at their sleeping son. "No matter what—"

Daniel hurried to fill the tense silence that followed. "It's been the best two years of my life."

"I thought you said *ten* years."

"I'm only counting the ones since I've known you—the year we were getting reacquainted, and the year we've been married."

She came to him then, and they cuddled on the under-sized hospital bed, comforting and encouraging each other as only a husband and wife can do when fear is like a living thing. They prayed their nighttime prayers together and then Daniel left, promising to be back early in the morning.

Once more Carole checked the baby to see that he was still breathing, and curled up on the bed next to his. Prayers and memories intertwined in her dreams as she half slept, listening for the slightest sounds Timothy might make. And when the alarm went off for his next feeding, it seemed she had not slept at all. She managed to wake him, but was frustrated at her inability to keep him awake long enough to nurse properly. She gave up.

"Timothy John Thornton," she whispered, hugging him closer, "what am I going to do with you? You have to eat so you can grow strong like your daddy."

She noted his tiny features, so achingly beautiful, so delicate, and tried to memorize them. "I've known you for almost a year now, but I don't know if you're going to get to stay with us. But God loves you even more than we do, and He knows best." She held his hand in hers, stroking the velvety skin. "You have a sister at home, too. Well, she's a half-sister, but she'll love you better than a whole one. I'm sure you've already heard that your dad is a pastor, and you and I have been to the bank where I work lots of times. I like being a counselor there, but I'm going to stay home and take good care of you for as long as you need me." She thought she saw a fleeting smile on his sleeping face.

"God has been so good to us, little Tim." She touched his miniature fingernails. "Your daddy can't wait to show you off at church. We'll get all dressed up on Sunday mornings and hear him preach. You'll love the music, and soon you'll know all the hymns." Softly she began to hum her favorite.

The dark night plodded on, and Carole continued to share her love and her faith with her child. Somehow this sharing helped prepare her for the actual possibility of having to give him back.

Sighing again, she gazed out the window, expecting to see deep blackness, but now there was a tinge of rosy gold on the horizon. She watched the colors deepen, fingers of the dawn staining the sky as the Texas sun began a hazy ascent.

"See, Tim, it's the beginning of a new day." Hope burst anew as a shaft of dazzling sunlight pierced the early-morning gloom. Was God telling her the baby could stay with them? "Thank you, Lord, for this special night and for today. Tomorrow is in your hands."

two

"I'm sure I don't need to tell you how well your son is doing," said the pediatric specialist on the eleventh day of baby Tim's life. "We're quite proud of his progress. So proud, in fact, that we're going to let you take him home today."

Daniel and Carole exchanged an excited smile.

"Can you tell us what was wrong with him?" asked Daniel, leaning forward in his comfortable chair in the doctor's office.

"Medically, nothing we can put our finger on, but we suspect a muscle in the esophagus was not fully developed at birth. All we had to do was keep your son alive long enough for that muscle to mature." The doctor gave them a big grin. "I know you're a minister. Well, God answered your prayers... and mine, too," he admitted. "Don't jiggle him around much, and burp him often. He's strong and healthy." He rose and extended his hand. "Go home and enjoy him."

"Thank you, Doctor." Daniel clasped his hand warmly. Carole's face shone. She grabbed Daniel's hand as they hurried out of the office to take their son home.

As they drove away from the huge hospital, Carole's happiness was tinged with apprehension which leaped to panic as she realized there would be no more nurses on call in the middle of the night if she needed them.

Looking over at his wife, unaware of her fears, Daniel smiled with contentment. "On our way home at last."

13

She gave him a brave smile. "At last," she echoed, and breathed a silent prayer that the Lord would make her instantly wise and resourceful.

Their home was in an older part of the city, where tall oaks and maple trees stood guard, unfurling their leaves like bright green banners to greet the new arrival. The house, set well back from the street, was a friendly brown brick with white trim. Its craggy face had seen many winters and, as if to get ready for the next one, gathered deep pink azalea bushes close around its foundation to keep its feet warm.

On the long white porch covering the front half of the house stood Leigh, Daniel's teenaged daughter.

Daniel grinned his big lopsided grin. "I think Leigh is eager to see you and the baby."

Carole waved. But despite her pleasure in seeing Leigh, Carole was nervous. She and her stepdaughter had reached a neutral place where Leigh no longer seemed to resent Carole's marriage to her father, but neither did she exhibit open affection for Carole. "I'm praying Tim will be good for our relationship. I can use her help right now. And her love."

"Let me see him," demanded Leigh as they reached the porch. She pushed back the lightweight baby blanket. "Oh, Carole, you did good! May I hold him?"

"Tim, this is your sister." Carole smiled as she handed him over.

"Who do you think he looks like?" Daniel asked hopefully.

"I think he has Carole's nose. Maybe *your* eyes and chin. But he's so tiny!"

"He didn't *feel* very tiny about eleven days ago,"

grumbled Carole, but she was beaming as Leigh carried the baby to his new nursery and placed him in his crib. He looked right at home.

"It's not fair I have to go off to camp right now," pouted Leigh.

"Hey, you'll only be a counselor for those darling children for two weeks," Daniel reminded her. "Think of it as a crash course in child development. Tim will still be here when you get back."

"You know," Leigh began thoughtfully, "this is a good deal for me. I get to practice on Tim and all those other kids." A mischievous glint shone in the dark eyes so like Daniel's. "Then I won't make all the mistakes you made, Dad."

Carole laughed at his mock indignation. "Since this is my first one, we'll learn together. After all, there's only *one* pro among us."

"And if you will look at my handiwork, you'll find her quite wonderful," he bragged.

"I quite agree," Carole said.

Leigh stood on tiptoes and kissed her father on the cheek. "One thing you did learn, Dad, was how to charm women."

"And I agree with that, too!" Carole's lips curled in amusement. "He certainly talked me into this fast-paced new lifestyle, complete with new family." She put her arm around Leigh's shoulder and drew her close. For once, her stepdaughter returned the warm pressure.

Suddenly Leigh pulled away. "Oh. . .I've got to call Georgianna right away. I promised to tell her all about Tim."

The door to her bedroom slammed shut, and Carole and

Daniel moved into their own room. In this private sanctuary, she stepped into the waiting circle of his arms.

"I've missed you so," he murmured against her welcoming mouth.

"I've missed you, too." She snuggled against him.

"Still worried about being a lousy mother?" He kissed the tip of her nose.

"Not me! I've had eleven days' experience! And I can always call on the old pro when I don't know what to do."

Daniel's stomach rumbled unromantically. "Sorry about that. I was so excited about bringing the two of you home this morning I forgot to eat breakfast. Allow me to lead you to the kitchen. You do remember the kitchen? At this very moment it is filled with all kinds of goodies from Tillie and Joyce. And," he announced grandly, "I have a momentous surprise for you that I will share during lunch."

"It's good to be home again where almost everyone is sane," she teased.

Carole was genuinely touched when she saw the bounteous buffet set out on the counter.

"That's not all." Daniel opened the refrigerator door and showed her the contents. "Look at all the food our people have brought in."

Her eyes sparkled. "Our congregation is so good to us. Food. Presents for Tim. And Leigh is being so loving. Life couldn't be any better, could it?"

"Oh, I think one or two things could be improved upon." The light in his eyes plainly told her his intentions.

"Yes, my darling. Soon." She kissed him lightly and began setting the table, then cocked her head, listening. "Is that the baby?"

"I'll check." He was back quickly. "No, still sleeping."

They weren't too surprised when Leigh stuck her head in the door and told them she was dashing off to have lunch with her best friend. Welcoming the unexpected privacy, they sat down together and shared the good food.

Carole took a generous bite of chicken salad. "Now about that surprise you promised me—"

He was practically rubbing his hands together in his delight. "Well, everyone from the church is dying to see the baby, of course. So I figured out a way to show him off to everyone at the same time. I've invited the whole congregation here to an open house!"

"You're kidding!" Carole was stunned. "When?"

"Oh, I wanted to give you plenty of time to get settled in, so I made it for Sunday afternoon." Daniel's air of complacency was fast being replaced with caution.

"*This* Sunday?" Carole gasped. "Three-days-from-today Sunday?" From the look of horror on his wife's face, Daniel knew immediately that he'd made a serious error in strategy. "Well, yes," he admitted. "But the morning Ladies Group is going to help. They'll bring the refreshments. You won't have to do anything but look pretty and show off the baby."

Daniel felt defensive now. The open house had been the easiest method he could think of to introduce his new son to the congregation. "Mrs. Charles will come clean the house and—" *Strike two!*

"Mrs. Charles! Daniel, you know what a snoop she is!" Angry tears threatened to spill over. "I don't want her around to check up on my housekeeping! Heaven knows what she'd tell everyone !"

"But the house is already immaculate. You even

scrubbed the kitchen floor the day the baby was born," he said reasonably. "I only wanted her to come in and touch up things." He was honestly surprised at Carole's reaction. "Darling, I'm sorry. I should have consulted you first. I was trying to think of an easy way to share our new joy, and this seemed ideal." He looked her straight in the eye. "But it's too late to call it off now. All the plans are in the works. I can't cancel out."

Carole's chin jutted out at him defiantly, but she acquiesced. "I know that. I'll have to make the best of it. Maybe Joyce can come over and help me before Mrs. Charles gets here."

The logic in that statement completely escaped him, but he didn't press for an explanation. "I'll help, too. Tell me what you want done." He was eager to smooth out the enormous wrinkle between them.

She frowned and shook her head. "Please just don't make any messes. Joyce will know what to do." She stood and took her half-eaten food to the sink, Daniel following close behind.

"I'm sorry, darling, I won't do this ever again, believe me."

She accepted his apology with a sigh of resignation. "It's all right. It will work out somehow." She softened a little. "Try to remember that this is all very new to me. I'm trying to satisfy someone's every need, someone I don't even know very well yet. And he can't tell me what he wants."

"I think you're doing a great job!" Daniel encouraged.

Carole's expression was grim.

But Daniel was determined to ease things between them. "Look, you nap while the baby sleeps. I'll put in a few hours of work at the office. Come on, Mom. I'll tuck you in."

As he drove to the church, Daniel marveled at his own stupidity. Viewed from Carole's standpoint, it was nothing less than that. *I'm not an old pro where Carole's concerned,* he thought.

He wound his way up the tree-studded hill to the stately white brick church that had been his unique place of service for the past ten years. Gum, pine, and oak trees shaded the entire area, and challenged the rising spire on top of the building with their height.

Entering his study brought a sense of serenity to his troubled heart. Here in the red-carpeted room with its dark paneling, he felt in charge of his life again. True, he had had his battles with individuals, but here he was the minister. God's representative.

His intercom buzzed and he settled down in the chair behind the big oak desk that had belonged to his father. "Yes?"

"I thought I heard you come in, Boss."

"Yes, ma'am, and what can I do for you?"

"Did you get everyone situated at home?" Rhoda's voice was cheerful.

"Ye—es."

"If you'll pardon me, you don't seem quite as excited as I expected for a new father."

"Anyone in your office?" Daniel asked. At her negative response, he invited her in for a quick cup of coffee.

Rhoda Blackmon had been the church secretary for close to twenty years, and had proven an invaluable asset to Daniel from the very first day of his time here. Now she was his right hand.

The woman knew every buried skeleton in every closet, but even the paid henchmen of the Spanish Inquisition couldn't have coerced her to reveal so much as the name of the current janitor!

She handed Daniel his cup and seated herself gracefully in one of the dark leather chairs in front of his desk. "Now, then, tell me what foolishness you've gotten yourself into this time." Her soft gray hair framed a strikingly attractive face, and she peered at him through fashionable glasses.

Things always ran more smoothly with Rhoda around. And Daniel sighed, relaxing a little. "To say that Carole was upset over my surprise is a slight understatement. I should have asked her about it sooner."

"Shot yourself in the foot, huh?"

"With a shotgun." He sighed again. "I'm so happy about the baby, but Carole is. . .well, she's different somehow since he came. I honestly don't remember Ellen being so uptight after Leigh was born."

"Daniel," Rhoda chided, "it's unfair to compare them. Besides, it's been too long for you to remember things like that accurately. Give Carole time to get used to being a new mother." Thoughtfully she asked, "Should we change any of the plans for the party?"

"No, I guess not." He thought of Carole at home. She was probably talking to Joyce at this very moment. Then the image of his son flashed to mind, and he grinned his crooked little-boy grin. "Tim really is a cute little fellow. Did I show you the hospital pictures?"

"Not for at least four hours," Rhoda said with a straight face. "Has he changed much?" At Daniel's slight blush, she added, "I'm glad you're happy about the baby. You'll be a good father."

She moved toward the door, crisply efficient once more. "Your phone messages are on your desk, and I added some appointments to your calendar—one tentative wedding date and the ministerial luncheon tomorrow. Oh, and Susan Lapney called. She was quite insistent about speaking with you. But when I told her you'd return her call, she said not to bother, she'd catch you later. That woman is a strange one, Daniel. Maybe you'd better be on your guard with her." Rhoda paused with her hand on the doorknob, and dropped her head to peer at him over her glasses. "You and Carole love each other. Be patient. Besides, you could do with some adjustment time, too."

Daniel's smile followed her out the door. He picked up the phone to call home, then replaced it as soon as he remembered Carole might be napping. For a moment he missed the carefree days when he could call anytime he pleased, just to hear her voice.   Daniel shook off his reverie and applied himself to preparing for Sunday. Thursdays were traditionally reserved for writing the first draft of his sermon. And by five o'clock, he felt satisfied with his efforts and cleared off his desk. He was looking forward to getting home. *Carole doesn't stay mad for very long.*

He entered the house through the utility room that led into the kitchen. "Everything looks normal." A small baby bottle half full of water had been left on the counter. The years rolled back and for a split second he was a very young pastor again, coming home to Ellen and Leigh.

Shaking his head to clear the memory, he called out, "Carole, I'm home." When there was no answer, he hurried to the nursery, calling again, "Carole, where are you?"

"Shhh! Will you stop yelling?" she replied in a fierce stage whisper. "I've just gotten the baby to sleep." She was laying Tim on his stomach in his bed.

"Why didn't you answer me? I was worried when I couldn't find you."

"I was right here in the room with the baby, Daniel," she explained very softly. "I couldn't answer you without waking him." She gave the baby a final pat and came to welcome her husband with a kiss.

Feeling like a rebuffed schoolboy, his ardor badly bent, Daniel returned the kiss somewhat perfunctorily.

"Come into the living room." She kept her voice low.

"Why are we being so quiet?" he asked, matching his tone to hers.

"Because I just spent thirty minutes rocking Tim to sleep, *that's* why."

"I thought babies were supposed to sleep through most anything." Daniel bit his tongue to keep back the retort that he'd never had to be so quiet for Leigh.

When they reached the den, Carole plopped down in her favorite chair. "Hmmm. This does feel good." She began enumerating the chores she had accomplished during the afternoon—the baby's bath, three loads of baby wash, sterilizing bottles.

Daniel listened, trying to appear interested in her report of total domesticity, but his mind was on dinner. *No signs of anything underway on the stove, and I have a meeting in forty-five minutes. Now how do I do this tactfully?*

"Would you like me to run out and get us some burgers and fries?"

Carole looked startled. "Oh, supper! Daniel, I forgot all

about it! And you have a meeting tonight, don't you? I'm sure there's plenty in the 'fridge. I'll see." She hurried out, apologizing again.

Daniel noted as she scurried away that she was looking more like his pre-pregnant bride each day. He longed to hold her close. Inhale the intriguing scent of her. Feel the touch of her hand on his face.

Impulsively he followed her. Coming up from behind, he wrapped himself around her, nuzzling her neck in his favorite spot. The kiss was familiar, the perfume was not. "You smell like baby powder."

"I know. I get it all over myself every time I change Tim. But it smells so clean, don't you think?" She turned in his arms and kissed him soundly. "Can you believe it? We're parents. Soon there will be school and homework and graduation, college, even a wedding." She was beaming.

"Whoa! The kid is less than two weeks old. Give him time." He pulled her closer. "*I* need some of your time, too."

"Hmmm. It's nice to be in your arms again."

He bent to kiss her, but she broke away. "Hey, if you're going to make that meeting, you need some supper right away." Hurriedly she put together a light meal for the two of them, for Leigh was out with Georgianna, as usual.

As they sat across the table from each another, enjoying cold chicken and a congealed salad, Daniel picked up the thread of their earlier conversation. "Darling," he began very earnestly, "I know you've just had a baby, and I'm not planning a full-scale seduction. I just want a little kissing, a little cuddling, that's all."

Carole dropped her gaze. "I hope you do understand." Then, on a brighter note, "Hugging and kissing I can handle."

"Then pencil me in for some hugging around ten-thirty, after I've made my calls," Daniel joked, his eyes shining with love.

He was home early. He showered quickly and dressed for bed, anticipating the joy of even a limited love life.

When he turned out the light in the bathroom, Carole was propped up in bed, reading a current book on child-rearing. "Listen to this—"

Deliberately, Daniel took the book from her hands, marked her place, and set it aside. "I've been counting the hours all day until this moment." He kissed the top of her head, lingering to draw in a deep breath. "I'm still not too crazy about your new perfume, though."

"Sorry. *Eau de baby powder* comes with the territory these days."

Crawling into bed beside her, he held her gently, stroking her face with his fingertips.

Just then a lusty wail sounded from the adjoining room.

Carole looked apologetic. "I have to go, you know."

Daniel heaved a mighty sigh. "Can't you tell him it's my turn?"

"Why don't you tell him, and bring him to me?" she suggested. "Bet you haven't put as many miles on your feet today as I have."

A moment later Daniel brought in their angry son. When he placed Tim in her arms, the crying stopped and the smacking began. "How often does he nurse?"

She grimaced. "As often as he wants. I feed him on demand, but I hope it won't be long before he's on a better schedule." She winced again. "Do you think I could get away with offering him a straw tonight?"

Daniel's hearty laughter startled the baby, and Tim opened his eyes. "Hey, he's looking at me! Hi, there, fellow. Do you know your daddy? Oh, you truly are a living miracle."

Together they watched their son enjoy his bounty as he lay nestled between them. Daniel's heart constricted with love as he marveled again at this product of their love. *A son. Part of me to carry on my name. I loved Leigh when she was born, and I was so proud of her. Still am. But there really is something special about seeing a replica of oneself.*

It was a special evening, one he would tuck away as a treasured memory. And as he watched Timothy's rosebud mouth receiving lifegiving nourishment, he felt only the tiniest twinge of jealousy in having to share Carole with so worthy a rival.

Only once before they slept did he think of his monumental blunder when he'd told Carole about his plans for the open house. *Well, Lord, you helped me out of the pit I dug for myself this morning. Now, please help me get through the party on Sunday without making any more dumb mistakes!*

three

Friday was a disaster. Daniel knew it was going to be when Timothy kept them up all night with his wailing.

Carole awoke feeling groggy and grumpy. And Daniel, equally exhausted and relying on Leigh to help with the baby, left for his busy day at the office, laden with guilt that he was deserting Carole when she needed him most.

The morning agenda was crowded, since his first appointment, a counseling session with the Wilsons, ran long. He had been working with them for several months now, ever since Polly Wilson's threatened suicide. Daniel was constantly amazed at the couple's lack of communication. Once he had asked them point blank if they ever talked to each other, expressing their feelings, except during their time with him.

Polly's succinct answer left no room for doubt. "It's safe here with you."

Daniel had encouraged them repeatedly to contact a professional therapist. He knew Ethan Stewart was well qualified, but they had flatly refused, saying neither of them was crazy.

Today Daniel decided to take the bull by the horns. At the end of a stormy tirade, when the couple had reached an impasse, he broached the subject again. "I've done all I can, but I'm afraid we're wasting everyone's time here. Dr. Stewart is a competent and compassionate man. His fees are reasonable, and he's agreed to see you." He handed Polly a small card. "Call him today," he ordered, "then let me know how things go with you. I'll see you Sunday." As he ushered them out the door, he added, "You will be coming to the open house, won't you?"

Polly Wilson, apparently relieved that the matter was settled, gave Daniel a grateful smile. "We wouldn't miss it."

Privately he wondered if she would ever find what she was looking for in life. Whatever it was, he doubted seriously if any one person could provide it. Perhaps Ethan would be able to wean her away from her fantasy world and help her recognize her husband's fine qualities before she lost him altogether.

"Why do you put up with me?" Polly had once asked him during a counseling session.

"Because I love you," was the straightforward reply.

And on that response, Daniel had bet all their future.

He rather looked forward to the next counseling session for a young couple soon to be married. The hour flew by, and as he used his professional skills, he was newly aware of how those same basic principles applied to his own marriage. Feeling a rush of adrenalin from the success of this encounter, he felt his love for Carole deepen and resolved to be more patient.

Daniel called her just before he went to his luncheon, hungry for the sound of her voice. "Hi, what's happening in the busy Thornton household?"

"What? Speak up, Daniel. I can't hear you over the baby." She sounded harried, and he felt a fresh pang of guilt.

"Everything okay? Why is he crying?"

"If I knew that, he *wouldn't* be. Can I call you in a little while?"

"I'll be at the pastors' luncheon—" He paused. "Uh
. . . should I come home?"

"No, I can manage. Talk to you later. Love you, 'bye."
The phone went dead.

He shook his head as he replaced the receiver. "I guess
she's all right," he said to his empty study. *I could go home
and help her. But Leigh's there.* Remembering Carole's
independent nature and his luncheon date, he chose the
latter.

It felt good to move among the other clergymen from the
various churches. He enjoyed the guys and reveled in their
camaraderie. Once or twice, he thought of Carole and
wondered how she was coping after her sleepless night.
But, of course, Leigh was with her.

When he reached the office he called home, only to get
a busy signal. "Probably talking to Joyce," he decided. A
feeling of loneliness crept over him and he dialed the
number again. The line was still busy.

Sighing, he checked his phone messsages and returned
several of them. Susan Lapney had called again, but she
would call him back, the message stated. "What could she
need?" he asked the mute telephone. "It must not be an
emergency or she'd have me call her." He tossed the note
in the wastebasket, but his eyes were on the clock, making
it difficult to concentrate on his work.

He was thinking about tonight. Fridays were traditionally the evening Carole and Daniel reserved for each other.
They had always done something together, even if it were
nothing more than staying home and watching television.
He was lonely for her companionship, her opinions on
church events, her touch, her love.

He tried to call her just before he left the office. Worry scuttled across his brow as he found the number still busy.

"The phone is off the hook, sir," the operator informed him.

What's going on? he fretted, then tried to reassure himself, *Maybe this is her way of keeping things quiet.*

Not knowing what to expect, he picked up some take-out orders from a Chinese restaurant and hurried home.

He was about to call her name when he remembered his earlier mistake. Quietly he put the food containers in the microwave oven and went to the nursery. Baby Tim was sleeping peacefully.

"I thought I heard you come in," Carole said, slipping into the room. He was surprised to find her smiling and relaxed. "You must be starved. Come to the kitchen and I'll find something." She moved out of his arms to lead the way.

"I brought supper home just in case," he told her. "Let's just eat the food I bought. It will give us more time together. Where's Leigh?" he asked, looking around for her.

"Don't you remember? She left today with Georgianna for camp."

Daniel groaned and held out her chair. "And I left you to take care of Tim by yourself . . . after last night."

"It's all right. I got a good nap while the baby was down."

Carole put the colorful cartons of lemon chicken, rice and snow peas, and egg rolls on the table and got out chopsticks and napkins.

Eyeing the chopsticks, Daniel made a face. "You know I hate to eat with these things. They leak."

"Come on, it's good for your character, Pastor Wong."

Daniel tried valiantly while Carole chuckled at his efforts. "You're sure in a good mood today. A little sleep is a wonderful thing."

"I had a long nap. In fact, Tim let me sleep all afternoon. And now, he's even letting me have a quiet supper," she said smugly. "He's been asleep for hours."

A half-remembered alarm rang in Daniel's head. "Oh, no. Sounds as if he's got his days and nights reversed. Carole, my love, I hope you've caught up on your sleep. It's going to be another long night."

No prophecy was ever truer. For the second night in a row, Tim was wakeful and demanding, leaving both of them zombie-like by morning. Fortunately, it was Saturday, and Daniel could sleep in.

"But what will we do if he keeps this up?" wailed Carole at breakfast.

"That's simple. Keep him awake today so he'll sleep tonight."

"You're so smart!" she shot back, short-tempered from lack of rest. "And who's going to keep *me* awake?"

"We'll take turns. I don't have to go into the office until afternoon. And Mrs. Charles comes at one to clean for the party."

Carole moaned. "I forgot about her. I'll never be ready in time."

"Don't worry. I'll help. But let's concentrate on Tim first."

They worked out a plan and alternated the care of the baby, keeping him awake as much as possible. When it was Daniel's turn, he found Carole in the kitchen, muttering to herself.

"All this time I've been tiptoeing around. Do you know that kid slept even though I ran the vacuum in his room, and played the radio *and* the TV *loudly*? I even moved him here in the kitchen while I straightened the pots and pans under the cabinet. He *slept,* for heaven's sake!"

"Motherhood is an ongoing education, my dear. Even if you have seven kids." His smile was forced.

"Bite your tongue. One is definitely enough."

"One never knows for sure, does one?"

She squinted him a look of pure defiance. "Saved by the bell," she quipped, hurrying to answer the front door.

Hearing Joyce's voice in the entrance hall, Daniel froze. He was still wearing his rumpled pajamas, and his escape route to the bedroom was cut off. *Maybe I can make it to the den,* he thought, and fled, only to be met at the door by an embarrassed Joyce.

She recovered her composure first. "Good morning." She eyed his summer pajamas as he edged past her.

Joyce's dark eyes were brimming with mischief and merriment in catching Daniel in this informal state. "You've got great legs, Pastor, but you forgot your clerical collar."

A blush colored Daniel's strong jawline, but he managed with as much dignity as he could muster. "If you'll excuse me, I'll just slip into something a little less comfortable."

He marched off down the hallway, to the delighted laughter of both women.

While Daniel was changing, Carole offered Joyce coffee as they planned the rest of the day.

"Mrs. Charles will be here around one o'clock." She moved the sleeping Tim around on her lap in an effort to rouse him.

After Carole explained why she was trying to keep him awake, Joyce volunteered for the job. "Why don't you go sleep? I'll mind the baby and ride herd on Mrs. Clean." She took Tim and pushed Carole toward the door. "Go on now. Rest. You're out on your feet. Everything will be fine."

In her exhausted state, even the coming of the world's best housekeeper no longer struck fear in Carole's heart. Dimly she wondered if Mrs. Charles would bring her usual cake. *I hope it's a spice cake,* was her last conscious thought as her head touched the pillow.

In what seemed only minutes, Joyce was shaking her awake. "Sorry to disturb you, Carole, but I've hit a snag I can't handle."

Recognizing her son's hungry cry, she reached for him. "Put him in bed with me."

Joyce handed Tim to Carole, and quickly there was blessed silence. "Are you hungry, too? Mrs. Charles brought snacks with her."

Alarm zigzagged through Carole. "Is she here?" she asked cautiously.

"Yes, she's washing windows . . . outside." Seeing Carole's concern, she added, "Don't worry. I did the laundry and your bathroom, and anything else I could think of to keep her out of your private life." Joyce plopped herself on the bed and shook her dark head. "She's a real workhorse, Carole. Where does a woman her age get so much energy?"

"It's fueled by curiosity," Carole ventured with a wicked grin.

The sharpness of the remark did not escape Joyce.

"Well, she didn't learn much here today."

Carole turned a grateful look in her friend's direction. "Thanks, Joyce, for guarding my reputation."

"There wasn't much to protect. Everything was in great shape." She couldn't take her eyes from the happily nursing baby. "He really is a beautiful baby, Carole." She touched Tim's clenched fist, and he promptly grasped one of her fingers.

"Yes, he is, one of the prettiest I've seen," agreed Mrs. Charles from the doorway. Her sudden presence startling both women.

Carole felt momentary embarrassment at Mrs. Charles's intrusion at such an intimate moment, but stubbornly refused to shield herself from the older woman's gaze.

"Seeing the two of you like that takes me back to when my mother nursed my little brother."

Carole was sure she saw a hint of tears in the faded blue eyes. "Come on in and sit down," she invited reluctantly, indicating her dressing table chair.

She and Joyce exchanged perplexed glances as the woman dragged the chair up to the bed. But good manners demanded the invitation.

"I do believe he looks like Pastor," Mrs. Charles said, before her eyes roamed over Carole's features. "But I think he has your nose."

Carole bit back her standard remark about her pug nose. Then she lifted Tim to her shoulder, gently patting him.

"Here," Joyce commanded, "it's time for your godmother to do her part. Let's get you some dry pants," she crooned as she took the baby from Carole.

Mrs. Charles's eyes followed Joyce and the baby as they left the room. "How lucky you are to have such a fine son."

"Yes, God has blessed us," Carole subtly corrected her.

Mrs. Charles drifted back into the past. "I only had one child," she said softly. "He was stillborn. I never even got to hold him." She swiped her hand across her eyes, brushing away sudden tears. Brusquely she added, "But you don't want to hear an old lady's sad tale on such a happy day. You're young and strong, with everything ahead of you."

Carole was deeply moved. Suddenly Mrs. Perfect Housekeeper was only a heartbroken woman who tried to cover her sorrow by staying too busy to dwell on it. She didn't even cringe when Mrs. Charles rose and took a dusting cloth from her apron pocket and began tidying the dressing table.

"I'll say this," the woman said, "you've certainly improved your housekeeping. Everything was quite nice when I came."

Carole smiled at the backhanded compliment. "Thank you. I try."

"Well, you're going to be needing some extra help now that you have a little one." She stopped in mid-dusting and turned to Carole. "Would you like me to come in once a week to help out? I could keep things orderly for you and Pastor." Her faded eyes were lively with hope. "You wouldn't have to pay me very much, just a little something."

Carole's heart sank at the naked longing she saw and, forgetting all the bitter feelings she'd ever had about the snoopy woman, found herself agreeing to the arrangement.

Joyce was standing in the doorway, her mouth open in a shocked "O."

"I'll just fix you a tray," Mrs. Charles was saying. "Now don't you move. I'll bring it right in to you." She positively bustled out of the door with the importance of her mission.

"What in the world do you think you're doing," Joyce hissed to Carole when the woman was out of sight. "Are you crazy?"

Carole sighed. "Yes."

"Well, I'm going home. I've seen everything now. You're on your own, kid." She glanced cautiously down the hallway. "I hope you don't live to rue this day."

"Me, too." Carole herself was still surprised by the unexpected turn of events.

"At least she can cook," Joyce conceded. "That spice cake was delicious." She eyed Carole's sudden laughter quizzically, gave a little wave of her hand, and left.

When Daniel came home at five, he was fed a good, hot supper by a beaming Mrs. Charles. He ate gratefully, but in the privacy of their bedroom, he quietly asked Carole, "What's this about Mrs. Charles coming in once a week?"

Carole shrugged her shoulders in puzzlement. "I'm not sure what happened, Daniel, except that she seems to need us. Did you know she had had a stillborn son?"

Wrapping his arms around Carole in a big bear hug, Daniel said, "Motherhood is becoming to you. On my last day on earth, I'd never have expected you to let Mrs. Charles anywhere near this house."

She grinned. "At least she can't complain about the way the house looks if she's responsible for most of it—" Thoughtfully, she added— "I hope."

four

Carole made no attempt to attend church on Sunday morning.

"No one expects me there so soon," she explained to Daniel. "And I don't want to mess up the 'almost schedule' I've finally gotten Tim on." She tried not to sound sullen when she said, "The open house this afternoon may do that anyway." Brightly she added, "But everything is ready. I'm going to keep the baby in his carrier. I don't want him handled to death. Remember what the doctor said."

"Fine," Daniel agreed, planting a kiss on the top of her shiny hair and giving the baby a pat. He was still eager to mend the slight rift caused by his plan. "You rest this morning if you can. And when I get home, you let me know if there's anything more I can do to help out. See you after church." He left in a cloud of spicy aftershave.

The morning passed uneventfully, with only an occasional guilt pang tugging at Carole because of her absence. She pampered herself with a long shower as the baby slept, then prepared her customary Sunday pot roast for Daniel.

"There, that should make him happy," she said as she slid the heavy pan into the oven. "I've made him something he really likes."

He was pleased. "Aren't you going to eat?" he asked as he sat down at the table alone.

"Not now. I'm running out of time and I need to bathe

the baby."

The timbre of her voice told him she was under stress. And it got worse.

Holding a slippery infant was still a new skill for Carole. She worked slowly, afraid she would frighten him, but Tim waved his arms wildly in search of something secure to latch onto. He didn't calm down until he was swaddled in his bath towel. He was cranky when she dressed him, and continued to fret while nursing.

"I haven't done anything right so far, have I?" she soothed as he alternately nursed and cried. "Oh, I wish you'd hurry up. It's almost time for this party to begin. Maybe you need to be bubbled." With the change of position, the baby promptly spit up the milk, getting some of it on Carole's new dress. "Oh, Tim! There's no time to change now." *Fortunately mother's milk doesn't have that icky formula smell,* she thought as she daubed at her dress with her new tool, the diaper.

The doorbell rang and Daniel hurried to answer it. Happy greetings and congratulations were exchanged, and the party was on.

Carole stiffened slightly at the sound of Teletype Tillie's strident voice trumpeting her progress down the hall toward her. Carole was seated in her rocking chair, cuddling the sleeping Tim when Tillie hit the nursery door.

The woman's flaming red hair was in stark contrast to the lines in her face. She was wearing one of her typical ensembles—red denim sundress, white straw hat, and immaculate white orthopedic shoes.

Tillie clasped her hands in pleasure as she advanced on mother and child. "Oh, do let me see that dear little thing," she cooed. "Why, Pastor, he looks just like you—" She leaned back in thought and put a finger to her pursed parrot-like lips—"except for his little button nose." She glanced meaningfully in Carole's direction, and Carole had to smile in spite of herself. "I don't suppose I could hold him a little while?"

"He's just gone to sleep, Tillie. I'm sorry."

At that moment dour Mr. Wilcott entered the room, but his face lit up in a silly grin when he saw the baby. " 'Lo, Mrs. Thornton. How's that little one? *You're* looking good."

"Mr. Wilcott and I just couldn't wait to see the baby," Tillie gushed on. "I'm so glad we were the first ones here."

Carole didn't miss the telltale "we" in Tillie's statement, and inwardly congratulated herself on having played matchmaker several months earlier.

The doorbell sounded again, and Daniel left to greet the other guests. His hearty voice could be heard inviting the newcomers to enjoy some refreshments before seeing the baby, and Carole welcomed the short reprieve after Tillie and Mr. Wilcott left.

For the balance of the afternoon she both endured and enjoyed wave after wave of visitors, diplomatically fending off all attempts to hold the sleeping baby. Finally able to sit still no longer, Carole laid him in his crib. And when Joyce brought her a cup of punch, she asked her friend to stand guard.

"As his godmother, you have the power to deny all requests to pick Tim up," Carole instructed. "And if he cries, *you* hold him, and hang on tight 'til I get back."

Carole made a quick tour of the den and kitchen where Mrs. Charles assured her all was well with the refreshments. The table was beautifully appointed, and Carole smiled her appreciation.

When Daniel caught up with her, he slipped his arm casually around her waist. "I do believe the entire congregation is here. What a nice turn-out to welcome our son."

She noted the pride in his voice, the pleasure reflected on his face, and she was ashamed of herself for being such a reluctant hostess. "Everything is going very well," she admitted lamely, trying to forget her stressful morning. Then she heard an angry wail coming from the nursery and gave Daniel a quick peck on the cheek. "Excuse me, I think that's for me."

Closing the bedroom door, Carole took advantage of Tim's feeding to chat with Joyce. She confided in her best friend the details of her day, trying to keep it light.

Joyce was sympathetic. "I've never had kids, of course, but my sister has six. She says babies pick up on the mother's nervousness. Tim probably felt your tension about the party. Guess I should have been here earlier to help," she said apologetically.

"You're here now. Thanks."

When someone knocked softly on the door, Carole called, "Just a minute," and pulled the lightweight blanket over her shoulder and the nursing baby. "A useful trick I've learned." She winked at Joyce. "Come in."

Tall George Williams walked in, smiling. Carole was glad to see the dignified chairman of the church council, and offered her hand in greeting. "Hello, George, I'm glad you came."

"Even bachelors love babies. Pastor says he's going to be pro football material." He leaned closer. "Is he sleeping?"

Before Carole could stop him, George reached out and flipped back the blanket, seeing much more than the expected sleeping infant. He let go of the blanket as it were a hot poker, blushed the color of a garden beet, and stammered, "I didn't . . . uh . . . I mean, I thought—"

"It's all right, George." Carole tried to rescue his dignity. "As soon as I'm through nursing Tim, you can take a good look at him. Please don't be embarrassed."

But all the disoriented man could do was utter a quick apology and flee.

When he was gone, the two women looked at each other and dissolved into muffled laughter.

"Oh, poor George, he'll never be able to look you in the face again."

"I'll bet he never looks at another baby, either!" Carole sobered. "I like him. I'm sorry he was so shocked." Looking down to see how the sudden laughter had affected Tim, it was her turn to be surprised. "Joyce, he's smiling at me!"

"See, even he thinks it's funny. You've got to put that incident in Tim's baby book."

Carole chuckled. "Wish I had a snapshot of George's expression." She handed Tim to Joyce. "Bubble him, will you?" She straightened her dress.

"Why don't you go back to the party for a while. I'll do guard duty." Joyce smiled.

Leaving her friend in charge of the nursery, Carole found herself gravitating toward the younger women who had small children. Before Tim, "baby talk" had bored her. Now she listened and compared experiences, picking up some sound advice. She was chatting with the others about the merits of sunbathing for babies when she caught

Daniel's eye across the room. He was deep in discussion with two men, but when he saw her watching him, he smiled secretively. She returned the smile, loving him more than ever as the father of her child.

Joyce came to fill the vacant spot beside Carole. "Mrs. Charles is on duty, all right?"

"I guess so."

Joyce leaned closer. "Do you see Susan Lapney over there talking to Daniel? Carole, I think she's flirting with him!"

Carole looked. Susan was hanging onto his every word, and her face was animated as she answered him. "She looks happy. Maybe she's telling him about Al."

"Her husband isn't that interesting. Sometimes she acts real spacy, but it may be a put-on. That helpless Southern lady thing. But I think there's a lot more going on in her head than she lets on. She's always dressed to the teeth, too. Even when we have our Ladies' Group. Guess you won't be there again this week, huh?" she asked hopefully.

"Joyce, you know the baby is too small to take out yet." Seeing Joyce's disappointment, she offered, "Maybe you could come by here for lunch. Saturday would be good."

"Yeah, that sounds like fun. I *don't* get to see you as much as I used to."

Carole winced. "You're not the *only* one who seems to feel that way."

It was late in the evening when the last guest left and Mrs. Charles finished up in the kitchen. Everyone agreed that Tim's debut had been an unqualified success.

In their bedroom Daniel thanked Carole with a tender kiss. "I know it was hard on you, darling, but you did well."

"Actually, it was easier than I thought it would be. I had plenty of help. All I had to do was smile and guard Tim." She began getting ready for bed.

A shadow crossed Daniel's even features. "Yes, a lot of people were hoping to hold him."

"And," she stated firmly, "if we had let them, he'd be bruised and sore by now." She turned to him, holding a nightgown in her hand. "He's only a tiny newborn, Daniel. People know not to handle new puppies or kittens, so why do they think it's all right to hold new babies?" Her whole being yearned for his understanding.

"I'm sure you're right." He dismissed the topic. "You get your shower. I'll check the baby. Can *I* hold him if he cries?" His face was mischievous.

The look she shot him on the way to the bathroom was mockingly venomous.

Tim was cross the next morning, and Carole spent most of the day rocking and feeding him.

She didn't feel housebound exactly, but she was finding the total care of a new child all-consuming. Only when Daniel was home or called, needing something, however, did she feel any conflict of loyalties.

Her love for her husband hadn't diminished, but her priorities had radically changed. *Thank goodness, he seems to understand,* she thought.

Daniel called from the office about one o'clock. "I'm taking the rest of the day off. Why don't we do something together?"

"Sounds interesting. What did you have in mind?"

"A drive to the lake, maybe?"

She laughed, feeling more like herself than she had in

ages. "I think I need some time out in the real world."

"Cabin fever?"

"A little," she acknowledged.

When Daniel arrived with the picnic items she'd asked him to pick up, he eyed Tim's large diaper bag with amusement. "Are we staying overnight?"

"No, silly, I'm just taking everything I might need. This is our first official outing, you know."

"You're well-prepared for any event," he couldn't resist saying as he hefted the bag in one hand, the picnic basket in the other. "Where's the baby?"

"I dressed him in the cutest little sunsuit. Wait 'til you see him."

The drive to Lake O'the Pines was pleasant with the air-conditioner on. Carole kept looking over her shoulder to check the sleeping child strapped securely in the back seat.

"Remember the picnic we had out here last summer?" Daniel was happily reliving one of the early events of their meeting.

"The storm, you mean?"

"No, the cabin where I first kissed you." Soft eyes of love searched hers for the memory.

"How could I forget it?" She leaned over and kissed his cheek.

"Safety belts! A hazard to love," he muttered. "Come sit in the middle and use that one. I want you beside me," he commanded.

Obediently she moved over, pleased he wanted her so close.

"That kiss in the cabin is what undid me," Daniel confessed. "From then on, I knew I had to have you for my own."

"I remember how you pulled away, leaving me totally confused," she countered.

"We've covered a lot of ground since then, though, haven't we?"

"I'd say so." She grinned archly. "That was barely two years ago. I'm sure we had everyone counting on their fingers when Tim was born."

"Never mind, love. *We* know the truth. And the Lord knows how we resisted temptation until we were married." He drew up his shoulders. "But I do work fast, don't I?" he bragged.

She gave him a sidelong glance. "I think I had something to do with it."

"Humph. If I'd left it up to you, you'd still be running." He ventured a quick look at her before returning his gaze to the road. "You're not sorry, are you?"

Laying her head on his shoulder, she snuggled closer. "No, my darling. I am totally content."

They pulled up to the picnic tables beside the roped-off swimming area and spread out a blanket under the enormous pine trees. A cooling wind sang through the needles and fanned the little family lazing below.

Reflections of sunlight, like the tinsel on a Christmas tree, floated off the water, bringing back vivid memories for Carole. The boat ride on the other side. The storm. Daniel's kiss. Her own rioting emotions. She smiled as she recalled Tilly's tight-lipped disapproval of the swimsuit some of the teenaged girls had been wearing that day, and later, the woman's ominous warning that a storm was approaching. How right she had been! There was a storm brewing, but it had reached its full magnitude in Carole's heart.

"She was right, in more ways than one," Carole mused aloud.

"Who?"

"Tillie. She told us a storm was coming. Remember?" Her eyes scanned the glittering lake. "I'd like to be in a swimsuit right now, zipping around in a boat."

"Yeah." He grinned appreciatively. "And I'd love to see you in it."

"I'm afraid it will be some time before I can wear a swimsuit again . . . if ever. The shape's a lot different this summer," she replied a bit wistfully.

"I still like the shape." Daniel moved to pull her against him.

"But I'm a mother now, Daniel," she protested.

"You're still my wife." He kissed her neck softly at the nape.

"Daniel—" Her serious tone halted his kisses. "I don't feel like a bride anymore. I feel, well, very grown-up and responsible. Yes, responsible, that's it," she repeated. "Until the baby gets to the point he doesn't need constant care, I just don't even think about, well, fun and games." She looked down at the baby sleeping in his carrier beside her.

"Fun and games, as you so euphemistically call it, was a vital part of our marriage." His voice held controlled heat. "At what point do you think he won't need constant care?" Before she could answer, he added, "I know this, a child will take as much time as you give it."

"But when he cries—"

"Did it ever occur to you that it would be all right for him to cry sometimes? Not if he's in distress or hungry, of course." His eyes bored into hers.

"No, I'm always afraid he needs something."

"That may be true of a newborn. But there will come that first time when you decide he can wait a minute and a half before running to him. And then the time when you've done everything, and you just have to let him cry himself to sleep." Daniel tried not to sound hard-hearted.

"I—don't know. There's always a chance something could really be wrong."

"There *will* be. What's wrong is that the baby has trained you well and has you on a very short leash."

Carole looked over at her husband with questioning eyes. "How can you be so sure, Daniel?"

"Experience, my dear, experience." He sounded tired.

Understanding dawned on her face. "You had this same thing with Ellen when Leigh was born, didn't you?" she asked softly.

"Yes, And it lasted a very long time."

"Oh, Daniel, I'm so sorry." Carole scrambled to put her arms around him. "And I'm making the same mistakes." She felt that same sense of confusion again. "Why do some women have such a hard time juggling motherhood and marriage?"

"Maybe because you're *too* . . . responsible," he said awkwardly.

She picked at the unexpected snag in the fabric of her life. "I'm glad we talked today. I still have a lot of things to figure out." She sighed. "Just when I thought I'd done some more growing up, you had to come along and now I feel like a kid again."

"I guess that means you'll be young forever." Daniel grinned. "But I want us to grow old and gray together. My own true love, forever," he whispered tenderly.

And when baby Tim began to cry, he swept up the child, laughing. "Yes, my son. It's your turn."

Despite her promise to herself and to Daniel, Carole still had trouble finding the right balance between husband and son. And each time she had to choose, she wondered if she had made the right choice. Life was much simpler when she and the baby were alone, and then she felt disloyal to Daniel for feeling that way. All her feelings were magnified a hundredfold each time she experienced his love for her in their most intimate moments, for then she knew where she belonged.

Still, those were the times she dreaded most. Daniel's expectant face . . . the baby's insistent cries.

"He's still so little, Daniel," she would say as she excused herself to care for him. And when she returned, more and more often she would find her husband asleep. Or was he?

five

Daniel sat in his study, enjoying the solitude. Rhoda had gone for the day and the entire place was still, except for the cries of the birds. At the bottom of the hill, he could see the late-afternoon traffic streaming toward home. But here in this green cathedral, among the stately trees, he was removed from the busy throngs.

The late summer sun filtering through the overhanging branches cast golden shadows on the newly clipped lawn as he stepped outside his office door. Following the walkway between the fellowship hall and the church, Daniel found a secluded step on which to sit and think.

He sat with his chin in his hand, and tried to put reason to work for him. *I've gone from being a widower with a daughter, to remarriage with a baby son. All in the space of two years. From empty to full to overflowing,* he concluded. *Talk about your major life changes!* Still, he loved Carole and his daughter dearly, and he felt enormous pride in having fathered a son. *I think they call this life.* He chuckled silently.

Even as he contemplated his problems, the beauty of the symmetrical trees marching around the property in their late summer lushness didn't escape his notice. A deep maroon-leafed Acer Maple, in particular, caught his eye. And the lemon-sweet smell of the overblown magnolia blossoms nearby filled his senses. He breathed deeply, savoring their heavy perfume. He let out another sigh.

I have some growing up to do myself. Patience has never been one of my virtues. He wanted his church membership to show growth more quickly—both spiritually and numerically. He felt frustrated at having to work everything through poky committees. He felt the pressure of time prodding him to accomplish his goals before it was too late.

And here I am with a teenaged daughter and an infant son, starting over again. Diapers and a baby crying in the night. Guiltily he wished away his son's babyhood to a time when they could do things together. *Or will I be too old by that time to play baseball and touch football with him?*

When he allowed himself an honest appraisal of his heart of hearts, he wished that he and Carole could have had more time together before starting a family. They had been at a good place in their relationship, getting to know each other on a more intimate level, sharing an ever-deepening love. Then had come the morning sickness. The middle months had been tolerable, but toward the end, her discomfort and plans for the impending delivery had occupied her every waking moment.

Still, that day in the delivery room had made it all worthwhile. A thrill of joy passed through him as he relived the moment of Tim's birth. Nothing could ever match the awe he had experienced that day, nor the fear when it appeared something was wrong. Then, after the baby was declared out of danger and Daniel had brought them home. . .well, Carole's absorption with their newborn had made him feel completely left out.

Lord, help me get a better perspective on my life. Lead me to be more patient with Carole and Tim. Thank You for

*the blessings of their love, and mold me into a good father
for Leigh and Tim, and husband to Carole.*

He heaved another deep sigh and rose to join the
commuters on their way to the suburbs. In only a couple
of hours, there would be another meeting back here at the
church. He'd have to grab a bite. He hoped it wouldn't be
leftovers again. Soaking up the serenity of his surround-
ings along with his prayers for strength as a buffer against
possible disappointment, Daniel squared his shoulders
determinedly and started for home.

But to his surprise and delight, when he walked through
the door, he found that Carole had planned a cozy dinner
for two. With Tim sleeping peacefully in his crib and
Leigh away for the evening, there was unhurried conversation over prime rib and potatoes. And when it was time
for dessert, there was yet another surprise. Carole led
Daniel to a mound of deep cushions in front of the fire
where she gave him her love as she had in the early days
of their marriage.

"Just like old times, my love," she whispered, nestling
against him.

Daniel, freshly groomed, walked toward the meeting
room of the church, trying desperately to wipe the smile
from his face. *Come now, old man, this will never do.
They'll read you like an open book.* He adjusted his
clerical collar and affected an innocent expression as he
entered the room filled with members of the Stewardship
Committee.

"Hi, Pastor, we were beginning to worry about you,"
George Williams called out.

Tillie's antennae quivered. "Anything wrong?" Her

sharp eyes pierced his.

"No, everything is fine," he calmly assured her. Daniel had dressed carefully and prayed mightily that he had left no clues to his recent activities, for Tillie was still scrutinizing him. "Let's begin with prayer." *That will at least get the focus off me and onto the business at hand!*

At the conclusion of the prayer he sat down next to Susan Lapney, a safe place, he hoped. "I'm glad to see you here tonight, Susan."

"Thank you, Pastor." She gave him a demure smile. "I'm glad to be here."

With a few opening remarks by the chairman of the committee, the meeting was officially underway. Its successful campaign in the fall would, to a large degree, determine the upcoming year's budget.

It was a spirited meeting, full of hopes and plans. Daniel was gratified by the enthusiasm and dedication of its members. Only at odd moments did a secret smile threaten to mar his pastoral decorum. And when the meeting came to an end, he felt energized.

Tillie, Susan, and Joyce stood around visiting, as Mr. Wilcott and George put away the chairs. Daniel spoke to them and to others who had attended, then helped the men briefly before making a quick getaway.

He congratulated himself on the way home for having moved from one role to another with relative ease. But he hurried, warmed by thoughts of Carole, eager to be with her again. And in the privacy of his car he made no attempt to stem the smiles that floated across his face as he relived the memory of their intimate supper.

The lights of his home had never seemed so welcoming as they did tonight, and as he and Carole got ready for bed, he knew that he had never felt so content.

Thank you, Lord, for my family. And thank You for making things so wonderful today. I'm getting Your messages. Patience. Hope. Love, he prayed, and closed his eyes to the noisy smacking of his son, who was enjoying a bedtime snack. For once, Daniel did not begrudge sharing Carole in the final moments of his day, and went to sleep with a big smile still plastered on his face.

His appointment book was crowded with meetings all week. Daniel was pleased to note that Susan Lapney was taking a real interest in the church's business. She seemed to turn up at every scheduled meeting. He also noted that Joyce was often with her, and wondered if the friendship between Joyce and Carole was cooling, now that the baby had come.

He felt better when Carole mentioned that the three of them were having lunch at their house on Saturday. "I shall make myself very scarce," he promised.

"That's fine. Mrs. Charles is coming in and she can help me with the baby." Excitement colored her cheeks.

"You're really looking forward to this, aren't you?"

"Yes, I really am. I'm beginning to miss my old social life," she admitted.

"Carole—" He caught her hand and pulled her to him—"I had a thought about Leigh and Tim today."

Her eyes widened. "Me, too. I think I know what you're going to say. It's a good idea, isn't it?"

He grinned. *"You* ask her to be a sponsor for Tim's baptism," he said graciously.

"We'll ask her together."

The baptismal date—the third Sunday in August—was firmly set and marked in Daniel's little red date book. "There. It's official."

"Tonight we'll spend the evening on the phone. I'll call my sister in Lubbock, too."

They made plans during their quick lunch, and Daniel left to make his hospital calls.

Daniel rather liked visiting his people, even when they were hospitalized. Few people in his parish did, however, and he was astonished to see Susan Lapney coming out of the room he was about to enter.

"Hello, Pastor." She flashed him an engaging smile.

"Well, hello! It's wonderful to see you here today." A little too heartily, he added, "I rarely have much help making hospital calls."

"Oh, I enjoy it. And I have the time." There was nothing extraordinary about her appearance, but today the petite brunette seemed more attractive than he remembered. *New dress maybe?*

Daniel sensed a kind of loneliness in her and was pleased she had reached out to others to fill it. "How's your husband?"

"Al's fine. He's on shift work," she offered. "That's why he doesn't come with me to church very often." She looked up at him earnestly. "He's not like you, Pastor."

"I'm sure he's doing what he can. He seems to be a fine man. Perhaps I should call on him again."

She nodded eagerly. "I'd love for you to visit."

On that note Daniel excused himself to make his rounds.

The days streaked by and Daniel was looking forward to

the formal dedication of his son to the Lord. And on Wednesday he took the day off to help Carole with the last of her preparations.

Mrs. Charles had come in early. As Daniel watched her prepare a sumptuous meal, he marveled at the transformation of Carol's former nemesis. Mrs. Charles still had sharp words for others, but she had become one of Carole's staunchest allies. And she absolutely adored Tim. She even scolded Daniel on occasion for his "messiness," but never once did he hear her say a cross word to, or about, his wife.

"Now, Pastor, don't you leave your newspaper scattered all over the den like that," she chided.

"I thought you got paid to pick up after me," Daniel teased.

"No one gets paid *that* much," she shot back.

"How can you be so cruel to Tim's father?" he parried.

"It's only biological, I can assure you."

"What?" Caught off guard by her unexpected remark, Daniel was more than a little mystified.

Never one to shirk her duty as she saw it, Mrs. Charles looked him straight in the eye. "How many times have you changed that child's diaper?" Before Daniel could answer, she hit him again. "I know you can't feed him often, but how many water bottles have you given him? Have you walked the floor with him, or kept him so Carole could get out by herself?"

"Well, I *do* have a job and—"

"Hmmph! I thought so," she muttered. "I'll bet you've never even given him a bath."

"Now, hold on, Mrs. Charles," Daniel began again.

"No, *you* hold on. It's high time you started being a real

father. This is a new world, and you have a wonderful opportunity to spend some quality time with your son."

Daniel's eyebrows shot up in total surprise, and for once in his life, he was completely speechless.

"I'll bet you're waiting 'til he's big enough to play football or baseball." Her normally faded blue eyes were blazing in the passion of her cause. Taking off her apron, she hung it neatly on its hook in the pantry. Her countenance softened a bit as she turned to leave. "Don't miss out on your chance, Pastor." And she was gone.

Dumbfounded, Daniel stood in the middle of the kitchen, unable to move. Words of protest rose to refute her statements, but they spun silently in his mind. Before he could recover, the doorbell rang in its sing-song fashion, signaling Leigh's arrival.

He longed to shout, "Time out! Wait a minute!" But Carole was already hurrying to open the door and welcome her home.

Leigh was obviously glad to see them as she simultaneously hugged Carol and exclaimed over the baby. When she saw her dad, she untangled herself and gave him a big hug and kiss. "Oh, Dad, he's more beautiful than when I saw him last. And he's grown so much!" And then she was holding Tim, carefully carrying him to the den and leaving Daniel to put up her suitcases.

"Welcome home!" he called to her rapidly disappearing back and struggled awkwardly down the hallway with her suitcases while Carole filled her in on the baby's vital statistics. *Here we go again,* he thought ungraciously. *She never gets tired of talking about him.* But by the time Daniel rejoined them, he was at least outwardly resigned to his place as second fiddle.

Leigh was totally enchanted with her half-brother. "Oh, look, he's smiling at me!"

Daniel waited his turn to enter into the conversation, but it centered on Tim, as usual. He stirred uncomfortably as Mrs. Charles's charges rushed back to convict him. <u>But</u>, he defended himself, *the baby is Carole's whole world. I can't do all those things for him and carry on my ministry, too.* A prickle of guilt burst the flimsy bubble of his excuses. *Well, I guess I could do a little more to help out.*

Sitting across from the two women on the couch, he watched as they chatted about his son. He had never felt the urge to spend a lot of time with the baby. The few times he'd held Tim had been enjoyable, but after a few minutes he was always ready to relinquish him to Carole.

This time, however, when Tim began fussing, Daniel was quick to ask, "Is he hungry?"

"No, just wet," Carole informed him.

Daniel sprang out of his chair. "Here, I'll change him so you two can finish your girl talk."

An astonished Carole handed over the baby. "Don't forget the powder."

In the nursery, Daniel carefully placed Tim on the padded table and reached for a disposable diaper. "This will only take a minute, little fellow, that is, if you'll cooperate."

Tim's smoky blue eyes seemed to be searching his face as Daniel kept up his small talk. "You'll feel so good once you're nice and dry." Feeling a little self-conscious about the one-sided conversation, he took time to marvel at the perfection of his tiny son's body.

Tim's eyes never left Daniel's face, and a fuzzy smile was the reward for his father's care.

"Hey, was that smile for *me*!" Daniel felt an unexpected surge of love. He finished the change and picked up his son, cradling him and stroking the tiny fingers. "Let's get a little better acquainted."

Daniel sat down with him in the rocking chair, supporting Tim on his lap so they were face to face. As he told of the dreams he had and the things they would do together, the baby responded with happy movements and lopsided grins, snaring Daniel's heart in a entirely unexpected way.

"Daniel?" Carole's worried voice drifted to him. "Is everything all right in there?" She hurried into the room, appearing startled to find Daniel and Tim in the rocking chair.

"Certainly." Daniel's happy grin was genuine. "Tim and I were just having a little talk—man to man."

"You were gone so long, I thought you might be in trouble." She was studying her husband curiously.

"Lady, you worry too much. We men can take care of ourselves, can't we, son?" And to the delight of all, Tim cooed in agreement.

"I guess now he'll be Daddy's boy, though I'm not too worried. There are still a few things you can't do!"

They returned to the comfortable den where, with diaper draped discreetly over her shoulder, Carole nursed Tim as they talked. Leigh sat next to her on the couch, and Daniel tipped back in his deep cushioned lounger.

"So, how was camp?" he asked, visibly relaxed.

"It was great, Dad." Leigh made a wry face. "I got that course in child development you predicted I'd get, and now I'm sure I won't get married until I'm at least thirty," she said dryly.

Carole and Daniel exchanged knowing looks. "Uh,

huh," they said in unison.

"I have a lot of school ahead of me," she said defensively. "I want my full education first."

"Good idea." Daniel nodded in approval. "Are you ready for next semester?"

Shyly Leigh looked toward her stepmother. "I thought maybe Carole could help me shop for some new clothes."

Carole gave her a quick hug. "I'd love to. Your father can baby-sit now that he and Tim have this new understanding." She blew him a kiss.

Daniel took up the challenge. "You're on. Just say when."

The next evening found Daniel conducting a Sunday school teachers' meeting. He was pleased, but not surprised to see that Susan Lapney had joined the ranks.

At the conclusion of the meeting, she stepped up to speak with him. "I really enjoyed having lunch at your home, Pastor. Your wife is so nice."

"She told me she very much enjoyed it, too, Susan. You're fast becoming invaluable to our church," he complimented her.

She blushed delicately. "Thank you. I'm just doing what I can."

"I know now that almost everytime I have a meeting, I can count on your being here."

Laughingly she admitted, "I haven't joined the choir yet."

"I'll bet it won't be long before you do."

She sobered. "Pastor, I like being here all the time, especially with Al working or sleeping. This church is like a big family, and I want to be part of it—" She made a sweeping gesture—"of *everything*."

Joyce called out to her, and Susan hurried to join her.

Daniel stood watching the two women as they chatted companionably, and felt a momentary loss for Carole. She should be here with her friends. Even after she had acquired her new job at the bank as an on-staff counselor, her social activities had never lagged.

He was also sharply aware that Carole was losing touch with the church. Once they had shared everything, had discussed church activities, the people, problems he encountered from day to day. He valued her insight, her observations. She had always been his biggest fan, his best support system. Now her interest in all these areas that so vitally affected him had definitely slackened, and he felt the void.

Her entire world revolved around one small baby, and most of the time, Daniel had to admit, *he* was still on the fringes of it. *Motherhood really changes a person,* he thought to himself as he gathered up his briefcase and Bible. *And I'm not so sure I like all the changes.*

six

Daniel eyed the package of round steak in Carole's hand as she put away the groceries.

"Chicken-fried steak tonight?" he asked hopefully.

"If I have time," she half-promised. "Or maybe I should save it for our anniversary supper this next Monday night," she said pointedly.

Daniel's mouth popped open in mock surprise. "Is *that* coming up already?"

Carole swatted him with a roll of paper towels, then put it away in the cabinet. "You know better! Did you buy me a fancy sports car?"

"Nope. A mink coat to wear to the grocery store." He pulled her into his arms, a package of pot roast trapped between them. "I do love your pot roast." He sighed. "You, too, of course."

She slipped the package into the freezer and snuggled closer. "You're so romantic, dear."

"I can be." He slanted her a sly look. "Actually I had in mind a very special dinner in a fancy Dallas restaurant."

Carole paused on her way to the pantry, a worry line furrowing her smooth brow. "But Dallas is three hours away, Daniel. That's too far to drive for dinner. . .unless we take Tim."

He sobered. "The reservations are for *two*, Carole. And I had hoped we could make it from Sunday noon to

Tuesday morning."

Her eyes clouded. "But I've never left Tim with anyone before. And I'm still nursing him. Oh, Daniel, I just couldn't."

Irritation was plainly etched on his handsome features. His lips thinned. "Never mind. I should have known it would be too complicated." He dropped his hands from her shoulders and moved away.

"Don't be mad at me, Daniel," she pleaded. "I'm not trying to make this difficult. It's just that—"

"It's all right. I just forgot for one crazy minute there are three of us now. We'll do something that won't be so. . . involved."

She hurried to make amends. "I'll make the steak, even fix strawberries and cream," she tempted him. "Or maybe we could try a sitter and go out somewhere nearby. . .just the two of us—"

Daniel was touched. She was trying so hard to placate him. "How about Leigh? She'd be pleased if we asked her to sit for the first time."

"Perfect!"

He brightened and pulled her close again. "That's my girl. We have some tall celebrating to do, you know. We've survived one whole year. And what a year it's been!" He gave a little chuckle.

"And it's not over yet. My sister is coming from Lubbock for Tim's baptism."

"Great."

"And her husband and three kids." Daniel seemed unruffled at her information. "And their St. Bernard." When his eyebrows rose slightly, she added, "And her eight puppies."

"I guess they'll have to use the den. The bedrooms are full," he responded stoically.

"You're no fun at all!" she complained. "I've already gotten reservations for them to stay at a motel. I was just kidding about the dog and the puppies."

He turned to go to bed. "I knew that."

"Actually they have a pet elephant," she called after him.

He kept going. "Better buy another can of peanuts, love."

She threw a hot pad at his retreating figure.

Daniel stood in front of the bathroom mirror, tying his tie. In their adjoining bedroom, he could hear Carole giving Leigh instructions.

"If Tim wakes up, you can give him some formula. Of course, you'll need to warm it. Use the microwave. There's a clean stack of pajamas in case he needs them, and you know where the diapers are kept. Let's see now . . . I put the doctor's number by the phone and also the number where we can be reached in case of an emergency—"

"Yes, Carole, I have all that. Please don't worry so. I've done a lot of babysitting, you know. Tim will be fine."

Carole laughed. "I guess I sound like a nervous new mom, huh?"

Daniel stepped into the room and nodded, grinning broadly.

Defensively she added, "Leaving him for the first time is hard. I feel as though I'm deserting him."

"I think you're a *terrific* mom. But I love him, too. And

this will give Tim and me a chance to get to know each other. Go have a wonderful time."

Carole gave her a grateful hug. "I keep forgetting you're a young woman now. I love you."

Leigh hugged her back. "You look gorgeous."

"Not like the mother of a new baby?" Carole peered at herself critically in the full-length mirror, smoothing her hand down over her slightly rounded tummy.

"You never looked lovelier," Daniel said, drawing her away from the mirror. "Now let's get out of here."

Carole was still giving one last-minute instruction as Daniel steered her toward the door.

The restaurant Daniel had chosen was the most expensive in town, and Carole felt a slight twinge of guilty pleasure as she walked into the tastefully appointed dining room.

"I'm impressed," Carole whispered to Daniel on their way to a choice table.

Daniel himself, wearing his best gray suit, felt a little like royalty with his beautiful wife, the mother of his heir, floating beside him in a gown of pale blue that enhanced her smoky eyes. Her auburn hair was piled high in a chignon, giving a regal effect. He would not have been surprised to hear a fanfare of trumpets announcing their arrival!

But it was only the maitre d'hotel who escorted them to a table overlooking a lush tropical garden. In the center a splashing fountain provided rhythmically soothing sounds. The room was bathed in candlelight, glowing in elegant wall sconces and chandeliers, giving the dusty mauve decor a romantic feeling. Deep maroon cloths covered small tables, flanked by plants, making each one a private island, drifting in a sea of muted music.

The waiter handed them an oversized menu and withdrew. "You look lovely in the moonlight," Daniel said with a private grin.

"The first time you told me that was when we were courting, and there wasn't any moonlight then, either." She laughed lightly. "But I still like to hear it."

"Let's don't quibble over details, dear. Have I told you lately that you are more exciting to me today than when we met?"

The waiter's return interrupted her reply. And after he took their order and left, Daniel's expression turned impish. "What I really wanted to order was chicken-fried steak and mashed potatoes. With strawberries and whipped cream for dessert, of course."

"Never mind." She smiled sweetly. "I'll make it for you later in the week."

When their salads came, Carole eyed the artichoke heart palm, basking in its rich dressing. "I wonder if this will upset the baby. I haven't eaten artichoke since I started nursing."

Daniel regarded her steadily. "Carole, I do have one request about our night out. Let's not talk about the baby. Let's just talk about us. . .you and me."

Her cheeks colored delicately at his reprimand, but she nodded in agreement. "Of course. This is our anniversary." There was a moment of silence as she regrouped and started again. "A year ago I would never have dreamed that we'd be sitting here tonight, celebrating a whole year of marriage." It was a safe beginning.

Daniel laughed. "I confess I feel the same. Things looked pretty bleak there for a while." He searched her face. "You're not sorry, are you? I mean, honestly."

"Honestly, I'm not. I've never been so happy in my life as I am with you at this moment." Her face was radiant, the smoky eyes reflecting the candleglow and revealing an inner joy.

"Carole, you've given me more happiness than a man has a right to expect. And with God's help, this is just the beginning."

He slid a small blue velvet box across the table.

Carole took it, eyes wide, and opened the box. Winking up at her from a nest of dark blue velvet was a pair of diamond solitaire earrings. "Oh, Daniel, they're beautiful!" she gasped. "You have to be the most generous and thoughtful man in the entire world." Her eyes grew suspiciously misty. "Thank you, darling."

"It seems they match the sparkle in your eyes right now."

Carole moved the jewels to catch the candlelight, admiring the simple platinum settings. "I just can't believe this. Daniel, I thought the wedding rings were a bit much, but now I must admit to you, I'm growing very fond of diamonds." She tipped her head. "Do you think I'm becoming too worldly?"

He chuckled with delight. "Only if you scheme for them. But these are a gift of love. In fact, there's a story behind them. They were an anniversary gift from my great-grandfather to his wife. He was a cattleman in South Texas, and it took a lot of hard labor before he was able to afford something like this. Talk about the lean years—"

He grew reflective.

Unmistakable tears pooled in Carole's eyes. "Oh, Daniel, I didn't think I could possibly love them more. But now—" She wiped her eyes. "Tell me about your great-grandparents."

"Oh, it's much too long a tale for one night's telling. I *will* tell you that they came from the Deep South to settle in the Promised Land. I have some old pictures in an album. We'll get it out one night and I'll tell you even more that you probably want to know—"

Warming to his story, Daniel continued. "My grandfather's name was Daniel Robert, and I'm told he was rather famous. Did a lot of good things for that part of the state. My grandmother was Mary Anna. She became the local doctor by necessity and inclination."

Carole smiled. "You come from good stock, darling. I know they'd be proud of you."

"Probably," he agreed unexpectedly. "If for nothing else than being smart enough and persistent enough to talk you into marrying me."

"Ahem, excuse me, sir," the hesitant waiter interjected. "Your dinner." He served the meal with a flourish. As he placed the final dish on the table before them, he smiled at Daniel. "I waited as long as I dared, sir."

Daniel grinned. "You must have an interesting job. Or do you get tired of waiting on tongue-tied suitors—"

"Sir, I never tire of hearing beautiful people declare their love. However, the chef does sometimes get testy when I don't serve his offerings at their peak."

"The chef definitely peaked this evening. The food is out of this world!" exclaimed Carole appreciatively.

"Almost as good as my wife's chicken-fried steak," Daniel agreed in a conspiratorial whisper.

The waiter left in the wake of their laughter.

So involved were they with each other that they failed to see Susan Lapney and her husband Al approaching the table. "Hello, Pastor, Carole," said Susan. Al nodded, and Daniel rose to shake his hand.

"You look so beautiful tonight, Carole," the younger woman said. "This must be a special occasion."

"Yes, it's our anniversary." When Carole saw Susan taking note of the jeweler's box, she explained, "Daniel just gave me a lovely pair of earrings."

Susan frowned. "You got diamonds for your anniversary," she said wistfully. "Al got me a washing machine for ours."

"I think that's a very practical gift," Carole said diplomatically, noticing Al's embarrassment.

"Pastor, you're so romantic." Susan eyed the diamond earrings once more. "Maybe someday Al will do things like that for me." By now her husband's usually ruddy complexion was turning an angry scarlet. "We'll be going now, Pastor," he said. "Hope you have a nice evening." He took his wife firmly by the arm and led her to their table.

"I can't believe she was so rude to her husband in front of us," said Carole when they were out of earshot.

"Yes, he was pretty hot."

Glancing in their direction, Daniel saw Susan watching him from across the room, while Al glowered. Then there was an angry exchange of words. Susan bolted from the table, her face crumbling into tears, Al following reluctantly.

"What in the world was that all about?" Carole wanted to know.

"I think I'd better mark a place in my calendar for some marriage counseling," Daniel observed. "Things sure don't look good for the Lapneys."

seven

The huge stained glass window in the sanctuary filtered streaming sunlight into a kaleidoscope of colors that splashed down into the congregation.

In the front pew sat Carole, holding a white-clad Tim, with Leigh and the rest of the family filling the remaining space. And during the opening hymn, Daniel couldn't keep his eyes off his wife and son. Carole's free-flowing auburn hair was deepened by the colors from the window, and she looked serenely beautiful sitting there. Never had he loved her more than at this moment.

He gave the invocation, then Carole, Leigh and Joyce moved with him to the baptismal font where they began the age-old custom of bringing his son into God's covenant with man. Though he had performed this ritual many times before, the hands holding his book trembled slightly as he read:

"Receive the sign of the cross. The Lord preserve your coming in and your going out from this time forth and even forevermore. Who brings this child to be baptized?"

Daniel looked at Carole over the font and they spoke in unison, "We do."

When he asked, "How is this child to be named?" Carole replied, "Timothy John Thornton."

And when Carole moved Tim over the font, tears sprang into his eyes as he poured the water of life over his son's tiny head. Tim looked up at him, but didn't cry out, and

Daniel wondered if he would even be able to utter the next words.

Only his professional training kept the ceremony moving smoothly, for the father in him was moved to the very core. Holding his hand over the baby's head, he prayed, "The Lord bless you, Timothy, in all your ways from this time forth and even forevermore."

Daniel was not alone in his feelings. He saw tears of joy in Carole's eyes, too, and as he handed her the baptismal napkin with which he had patted Tim's head dry, the look of pride and love they exchanged threatened to undo him entirely. Struggling to regain his composure, he threw himself into the liturgy, sure that no one but Carole could know how profoundly he had been touched.

His sermon went well, and then the people were converging on him from every direction, offering congratulations as he shook hands with them at the door. He felt exuberant and invincible, loving and beloved, the shepherd among his flock. He saw not a single face that day that was not dear to him.

Only when Susan Lapney came to shake his hand did a slight frown cross his features. But she was cheerful and effusive in adding her congratulations, and this was certainly not the place to ask her about her fight with Al.

Carole stood beside him, Tim safely strapped in his carrier, sharing the good wishes of the people. Leigh received her share as well, and Daniel heard her handling the comments with grace. *We really are a family. What more could any man have, or want?*

When they reached the house, the Texas sun was blazing in the August sky, but the wind had mercy on them and blew cooling breezes under the shelter of the patio, where two large tables had been set up to accommodate the family gathering.

Mrs. Charles bustled about, setting out a huge charcoaled brisket and all the trimmings. She was putting a serving spoon in the mountain of snowy potato salad when Daniel drew her aside.

"May I have a word with you? You've become an important part of this family, you know."

"Oh, Pastor, go on with you." Her pleased smile contradicted her denial.

"And I want you to know I have taken seriously what you said to me the other day. Thank you." He gave her an affectionate hug.

She gave herself up to a big sniffle. When he released her, she used the hem of her apron to daub her eyes.

"Now what's your first name?" Daniel went on. "I can't continue to call one of my most trusted advisors and the hub of my household 'Mrs. Charles'?

The glow on her face could have illumined the coming night. "It's Pearl."

"Pearl," he repeated. "It fits you, for you truly are a jewel to us." With a twinkle in his eye, he added, "However, the red beans could do with a little more salt."

"Pastor," she said, shaking her head, "you're hopeless."

Daniel grinned. "That's exactly what my wife says!"

Joyce approached at that moment, carrying Tim. "Here's your papa. It's your turn," she said to Daniel as she handed the baby to him. "We're all trying to get the food on the tables."

"My pleasure." He winked at Pearl. "Tim and I have been spending a lot of time together. I even gave him his bath last night. I also gave him a few pointers on football.

Look at those muscles. He'll definitely be ready by September. My main problem will be finding a uniform to fit him. Do you sew, Pearl?"

"Luckily for him, no." She hurried back inside, stopping only to hold the door open for Carole, who was coming out with a steaming bowl in her hands.

"I hope we have enough food," she worried aloud, and set the bowl of beans on the table.

Surveying the feast, Daniel tried to be helpful. "Maybe we should put out the bologna, just in case."

She ignored him, of course. He watched the scurrying women add more goodies to the heavily laden table. "Hey, this baby-sitting is a good deal. No wonder women have babies. Gives them an excuse just to sit around."

At this outrageous statement, she sliced him a murdeous glare.

When at last everyone was seated, Daniel prayed, and then spoke briefly, thanking each of them for sharing their joy.

A burst of laughter followed the comment of one of Daniel's nephews, when the child asked in a loud voice, "Is he going to preach again, Mama?"

Waiting for the outburst to die down, Daniel grinned. "No, son, I'll spare you. Besides I don't get paid for preaching at home." He considered for a moment, then said, "The best sermons are God's people living out His plans for them in His footsteps."

With that, he sat down and began passing the food.

Daniel's face was shining like a lighthouse beacon in a storm. "Wish I could keep this mountaintop feeling forever," he confided to Carole.

She cocked her head. "You know that's a direct dare to

the devil. He won't be able to pass up that challenge. He's probably sending old Screwtape right now to tempt you."

"I read that book, too, my love. And I'm ready for him today."

"There's always tomorrow," she reminded him with a wicked grin.

But Daniel promised himself he would do everything he could to hold fast his joy. And that night he went to bed with a smile and a prayer of thanksgiving in his heart.

Daniel awoke the next morning at his usual time, without the aid of the clock radio, and then closed his eyes gratefully and rolled over with a sigh. I love Mondays. It was his well-earned day off, and there was no need to hurry out of bed.

Carole was sleeping soundly beside him. He moved over to cuddle with her, inhaling the fragrance of her hair as he put his head on her pillow.

"Don't, Daniel," she mumbled irritably. "I was up half the night with the baby."

"Sorry." At her rebuff, he moved back on his side of the bed, disappointed, but trying to be understanding. He scrunched down the pillow and tried to go back to sleep, but it was useless.

Knowing that Carole needed her rest, he slipped quietly out of bed, checked on Tim in the nursery, and went to the kitchen to get a cup of coffee. He took both the coffee and the morning newspaper out on the enclosed terrace off their bedroom.

The huge old magnolia tree gave shade and fragrance in equal measure. It would bloom well into September. He settled into the lounger, thoroughly enjoying the relative coolness of the morning.

He had finished reading the sports section when Carole joined him, coffee cup in hand. She leaned down to kiss him. "Sorry I growled at you, but I had a bad night with Tim."

"I'm sorry I didn't hear him and help you." He was pleased to see her in a conciliatory mood. Things were looking up. "Here, come sit beside me in the lounger."

"It's too small for both of us."

"Maybe we'll have to sit really close together," he suggested hopefully.

She laughed at his air of mock innocence and started walking toward him when a loud wail sounded from the nursery.

Daniel leaned his head back against the cushioned chair. "So much for early-morning conversation. I thought maybe it was my turn again."

She halted in her tracks. "Daniel—"

He waved her on. "I know, I know. Go on and take care of Tim."

She disappeared into the house.

Strike two. This day certainly hasn't gotten off to a very good start. He knew he was being unreasonable, but he felt grumpy. He could feel himself slipping off the crest of the mountain.

Carrying the paper with him into the house, he took a certain amount of perverse pleasure in dropping it carelessly beside his lounge chair in the den. *I wonder if Pearl's coming in today?*

At noon Rhoda called. "I hate to bother you on your day off, but I have some important mail for you."

"An emergency?" Daniel mentally prepared himself to

rush somewhere.

"No, but I've worked too many years in a church office not to recognize a call to another church when it comes. Maybe it's the big brown mailing envelopes they always use."

"A call? Are you sure? Which church?"

"Yes, no, and I'm not positive," she answered his questions in sequence. "The name of the church is. . .no, I'm not going to tell you. It's too much like opening someone's birthday present. I'll drop it by in a few minutes. I'm on my way to lunch."

He opened the door almost as the bell sounded.

Rhoda handed him the bulky envelope with a grimace. "I'm certainly not glad to give this to you. Just remember you're doing a fine job here, and we still need you."

Her words were semi-serious, and she shook a warning finger at him.

His eyes sped to the left-hand corner of the package.

"I know it's a bigger church," Rhoda continued, "but the way we're growing, we'll pass them in no time with you as our pastor." Softly she added, "I'll remember all of us in my prayers while you decide where you think God wants you." She left before he could think of an appropriate answer.

"Who was that at the door, Daniel?" Carole called from the den.

"It was Rhoda." He headed toward her, carrying the unopened missive.

Her eyes widened in surprise as she recognized the package he held in his hands. "Daniel?"

He sat beside her on the couch. He knew God might be offering him the opportunity to serve at another church.

Taking out the official letter informing him that St. Paul's had met and had unanimously voted to extend him a call to be their minister, Daniel scanned it. Information on salary and church statistics were included. There were photographs of the church and brochures on the city. All in all, the call presented a tempting challenge.

Daniel was quiet as he absorbed the array of information, handing the printed material to Carole as he completed it. She kept still, respecting his need to grapple with the immensity of what this call could mean, before discussing it with her.

"It's a very large church," she finally said, looking at him and trying to read his reaction.

"Yes. It offers ample opportunities for my ministry."

They both knew many days of prayer and consideration were ahead for him.

"Well? What's your initial feeling?"

"It's definitely something to think and pray about." He leaned back into the deep cushions thoughtfully. "Every time I get a call to another church, though, it's a shot in the arm. No matter how well or badly things are going, it's an ego boost to know that someone, somewhere, wants you. The first thing I must do is notify St. Paul's that I've received the call letter, then I'll call George Williams and tell him, too."

Carole smiled as he rose. "You're well loved here, darling. I doubt that anyone will be pleased to hear this news."

"Oh, I'm sure there are a few. There always are."

Moving to the phone in the kitchen, he dialed the number of the interim minister at St. Paul's, who gave quite a sales pitch. Daniel couldn't help feeling a surge of excitement, but he gave only his promise to pray and consider the call seriously.

And when he spoke with George Williams, there was no doubt as to his feelings about it. "I'd hate to see you go, Pastor, but I know you must decide where God wants you to serve. I'll notify the others on the council, and we'll all be remembering you in our prayers."

Daniel felt the unfolding of a familiar ritual. His call would spread by word of mouth, but it would be announced officially both in the Sunday bulletin and orally at the close of the church services.

He would begin to look with searching eyes at his ministry here, its strengths and weaknesses. And finally he would have to decide where he could serve most effectively. Though at this moment he was not inclined to leave, he had to weigh all the possibilities honestly. Then, no matter how sad the parting, he might have to go, for his ultimate commitment was to serve his God...wherever He called.

eight

Carole sat in the deepening shade of their walled-in garden, nursing Tim and contemplating the future. *I really don't want to go,* she decided. Suddenly she loved her home more than ever, the people at the church, the town.

Her practical nature dreaded the thought of packing, tearful goodbyes, relocating—all the changes that come with starting over. With new awareness she thought, *I want to stay in my green haven forever. There has been so much love here.*

This is where she had come to begin rebuilding her shattered life after Samuel's death. Here, for the first time since she'd married the young minister, she had been just another member of the congregation. It had been a delicious feeling. For a while she had been no longer the center of attention. . . nor the target of criticism. She had actually begun to find some peace. Then Daniel had come rushing into her life, demanding her love and flooding her with his.

She smiled as she remembered their very brief, very intense courtship. It had been a battle of wills from the beginning. Her hesitation in marrying another minister and the life that went with that was something she had carefully avoided. But Daniel's love was all-consuming . . . and now she had a wedding ring and a child to show for it. No, *two* children, she quickly reminded herself, though Leigh was hardly a child anymore. *So much happiness.* She gave a little sigh.

Knowing the depths of Daniel's love for her, Carole was aware that if she flatly refused to move, he would return his call. In her wisdom she also knew she had no right to make that decision for him. God had called Daniel, and in His own way, He had called her, too. Together they served the Lord. She would go where He led them. *But right now, Lord, I'm hoping we can stay here,* she whispered into the blue sky.

Moving inside, she went to the nursery and lay Tim in his crib. "I'll get it," she called to Leigh when the phone rang.

"What's this I hear about Pastor getting a call to another church?" demanded Teletype Tillie.

Tillie's early-warning system has never failed her, mused Carole. "Yes, he did."

"I don't suppose he's decided anything yet, has he?" Hope for the juicy details rode high on Tillie's question.

"No, he's only had the letter for a few hours." Carole bit her tongue to keep from asking how Tillie had found out so quickly.

"It's a bigger church than ours, isn't it?" Tillie plumbed a little deeper.

"Yes." Carole smiled as they played the game, knowing that Tillie was the one squirming on the hook.

The determined woman worked a little harder. "Such a temptation for a young pastor. Moving on up the ladder." Tillie sighed and waited. When Carole didn't offer to reply to this rather inflammatory remark, she tried again. "I know I'm suppose to pray that he goes where God wants him. But I'm goin' to pray that he stays right here. You, too, of course."

Carole was genuinely touched by the backhanded compliment. "Why, thank you, Tillie." Knowing that whatever she said would be instantly passed on, Carole was careful to guard her own feelings. "Just as you said, we'll just have to wait and see where the Lord wants him."

"How's everything goin' for you and the little one? We don't see much of you at the church anymore."

"We're fine." Carole didn't rise to her bait, refusing to defend the way she spent her time.

But Tillie came through. "I guess a new baby does take up most of your energy. I remember when our first one was born. Had a terrible time. Did I ever tell you about that?" Before Carole could respond, she launched into one of her favorite subjects—horror stories of childbirth. "I was in labor three days. It was just awful."

To avoid the inevitable, Carole made a quick decision. "Tillie, I'd really love to talk with you, but I think I hear the baby crying. Thanks for calling, and I'm pleased you want us to stay. See you later. 'Bye." With this "little white lie," Carole's conscience gave a mighty tug. *I'm sorry, Lord, but surely you don't require me to listen to that again. I'm just too tired to hear another "organ" recital today.*

She checked on the sleeping baby, then started a load of wash. Even with Pearl helping out with the housework, there was always laundry to do these days.

A glance at the clock told her it was almost lunch time. Opening the refrigerator, she shopped for a light meal. *There's meat loaf from last night. Hmm. Meat loaf sandwiches.*

"Need some help?" Without waiting for an answer, Leigh began setting the table. "What are we having for dessert?"

"I think there's some chocolate chip. I got it just for you."

Her stepdaughter's smile brought a warm wash of happiness. They'd come such a long way together since the early days of their relationship, Carole thought with immense relief. Their old competition to be first in Daniel's heart had diminished with time and Tim's arrival. And Leigh seemed content to live with them. At least for now.

When they heard Daniel's car drive up, Leigh went outside to meet him. Father and daughter entered shortly afterward, carrying sacks of groceries.

Daniel grinned. "I thought we could use a few things."

"Thanks, dear. But I already have your lunch ready."

Noting the menu, his grin slipped a degree. "Meat loaf again?"

Carole was immediately defensive. "There was too much to throw away."

"If you eat a good lunch, Dad, you can have some of my ice cream for dessert," Leigh said gleefully.

"No fair! I'm outnumbered!" Daniel grumbled and joined them at the table, bowing his head for grace. "For what we are about to receive. . . *again*. . . we thank you, Lord."

"Dad," Leigh began as they ate, "how long do you think you'll need to make up your mind about your call?"

"Why? What's the hurry?"

"Oh, I was just wondering." Absentmindedly, Leigh pushed some potato chips around on her plate. "I was trying to figure out what I'd do if we moved. About college, I mean."

"Don't worry about it yet. We have plenty of time. And, I promise, you'll be one of the first to know," Daniel assured her.

"That reminds me," Carole injected. "Tillie called. She'd like a quick answer, too. She's right on top of things. The major networks are missing a good thing in not hiring her."

Daniel smiled at her careless assessment of the church busybody. "Maybe I should tell her my wife serves me dead meat loaf sandwiches for lunch."

"You do, and I'll tell her you have a pair of shorts with little hearts on them," she threatened.

"You guys, honestly," complained Leigh. "Why can't you act like normal married people." But a slight smile betrayed her real feelings.

Later that evening, Carole found Daniel working at his desk in the study. "What are you doing in here all my yourself, dear?" she asked, looking over his shoulder at a sheet of paper which he had divided into columns.

"Measuring. On this side I've put my strengths and on this side, my weaknesses. Here I've listed what I've already accomplished at the church and over here, what I hope yet to do."

"I'm impressed."

He swiveled in his chair to look up at her. "Carole, I'd like to make a trip to St. Paul's, talk with the people, get the feel of the place. I can't weigh what I don't know. And letters can't give me all the information I need to make a decision this important. Will you come with me?"

"Oh, Daniel, I don't know. The baby—"

"You don't have to tell me. . . you don't want to leave

him yet."

"I *can't* leave him. He's not weaned. How hard would it be to take him with us?"

Daniel pulled her down into his lap. "That could be hard on everyone. But we don't have to go tomorrow. Maybe next week. We could make it our anniversary trip."

She struggled to find the words to explain her reluctance to leave Tim in the care of someone else for several days. "I don't want to wean him yet, Daniel. He's still so little."

"Well, will you at least think it over?" He sounded beaten as he added, "We can talk about it tomorrow night."

It was very quiet as they prepared for bed.

Daniel was warm and loving, though, as he pulled her into his arms. Carole resisted his coziness. Her husband had released a turmoil of conflicting emotions in her, but passion was not one of them.

"Good night," he said and kissed her tenderly.

But the kiss she gave back left no question that it really meant good night.

He released her, sighing, and turned over to his side of the bed.

It's too late tonight to explain, she thought wearily. *He drops this trip on me, then expects me to fall into his arms. Men are so strange. Doesn't he understand? Lord, help me figure out what to do. Please show me how to juggle the roles You've given me.*

She awoke, tired and listless, her problem unresolved. Daniel had already showered and shaved and was eating breakfast when she joined him in the kitchen.

"Good morning." He looked up from his cereal with a tentative smile.

"Morning." Her light kiss was one of apology.

He made no attempt to resurrect last night's discussion, and she was relieved. Neither did he seem angry about the unsatisfactory conclusion to the previous evening.

He took a bite of his cereal. "I miss your pancakes."

Carole heard an accusation in the statement. Her first impulse was to lash out at him, but she felt herself on tenuous ground after last night, and she chose a meek reply instead. "I don't cook much for you anymore, do I?"

"No. I understand why, but I still miss all the time and attention you used to give our meals." He didn't lift his head to look at her.

"Do you feel I love you less, because I don't cook for you?" They were in serious waters now.

Idly he stirred his cereal. "I know you still love me. I guess I miss being fussed over." He saw that his honesty blistered her.

But she wasn't a quitter. "Our life has changed radically since Tim came. Daniel, I do the best I can. I haven't learned how to be a mother and a wife without cheating one of you." Her voice was almost a whisper. "I'm sorry."

"I know." He sounded resigned. "I'm sorry, too." He passed his hand across his face, rubbing his eyes. "There's so much adjusting to do. I honestly don't remember going through all this with Ellen when Leigh was born."

"Maybe Ellen was a much better manager, a much better wife—" Her reply was just this side of sarcasm.

"I didn't say that, Carole. I said I don't remember feeling left out for so long."

"No, what you said is that you didn't feel loved because I don't take care of you." She was getting angry, and her voice rose. "Do you honestly believe that? If you do, then you'd better examine how you've been measuring my love. If that's the ruler, then remember the special meal in front of the fireplace, and the extra care I took to put Tim to sleep so we could be alone. Remember?" She was in a full-flowered rage now. "How dare you say I don't love you because I don't cook for you!" Angry tears sped down her cheeks.

"I didn't say that." Daniel's tight-lipped retort was delivered slowly and deliberately. "I said you aren't showing your love for me the way you used to... yesterday morning and last night being prime examples."

"That's not fair. I told you I had been up half the night with Tim."

"Nevertheless, it's a fairly accurate picture of the way things have been going around here lately." His voice took on a more conciliatory tone. "All I want is time for *us*, Carole. Time to love and laugh and share. The only thing we ever discuss is the baby."

His hand reached for hers across the table. "Carole, look at me." Obediently she lifted her eyes to his, her chin jutting out defiantly. "I know Tim takes a lot of your time, but *I* need you, too. I promise to be more patient, but I'm hoping it won't be long before I'll be first in your life again."

Carole was stunned by his confession of loneliness. She was also angered by the implication of his words. "I should think a mature man would understand that this is only temporary. Tim won't be tiny forever. He'll need less and less of my time. But right now I owe it to him to give him the best start I can—" She leveled a long look at him— "even if I have to 'choose' him over you. I'm sorry if that hurts you."

Carole's firm words were a reprimand. She felt Daniel recoiling, retreating.

"What hurts me is that things can't be the way they were," he said after a lengthy silence. "The baby was supposed to bring us more joy, not divide us. But *he* isn't dividing us. It's *your* perception of motherhood." He rose from the table and looked at her squarely. "I can see we have some tough years ahead of us if you don't change your attitude. You've got to learn to mother Tim, not smother him. I love you, and I'll wait for you. But, remember, I'm only a man. Don't make me wait too long."

She watched him turn and walk out the kitchen door. Heard the side door close a little too firmly behind him. Heard him start the car. Only then did she release her pent-up emotions. Tears of rage, injustice, fear and impotence streamed down her face. Grabbing a hapless kitchen towel, she alternately twisted and pounded it, venting all the turmoil inside her. She didn't try to sort out her feelings, she just let them explode from her. And when she was through crying, she found herself in a strange calm.

Eye of the storm, she mused. Intellectually she could look at Daniel's charges and recognize many of them as true.

I do talk about the baby too much. He's my whole life right now. That thought chilled her, for it supported Daniel's claim of neglect. Once *he* had been her whole world. *But Tim is so little,* she argued.

I should cook for him more, she decided. *At least I can make some of his favorite desserts until things get back to normal.*

But the hardest charge to face was the one about her losing interest in his work. She rarely asked him about parish activities anymore, nodding vaguely when he told her about another meeting, and thinking that meant trying to hurry something together for a quick supper.

Guiltily she thought of the many Sundays she had not shared with Daniel in the worship service. There could be no discussion on the text or critiques of his delivery afterward.

It's too true, she thought miserably. *Tim is the center of my world.*

She allowed herself to relive the honeyed early days of her marriage. Viewed from this perspective, she, too, felt a little restless. And her restlessness mirrored Daniel's discontent.

Now was the time to consider some careful options. *I must find a way to balance my life. But it can't ever be like that again,* she thought miserably. The soft rainbow-colored memories crumbled in the face of another reality. *We're a family now.*

So how do we recapture the old times? she pondered. A baby-sitter for Tim seemed an obvious answer. *I'll do it.*

With a flash she remembered that this was the evening she was to tell Daniel whether or not she would take the trip to St. Paul's with him. Panicked at the thought of having to carry out her recent resolution so quickly, she gasped softly, "I can't!" *Not yet, Lord,* she prayed silently. *Please give me a little more time.*

nine

Daniel stopped just short of slamming the door as he headed for his car. His hand was trembling with anger as he jammed the key into the ignition and roared off toward the church.

He noted that Rhoda's car was still not in her usual parking space. Good. He needed to be alone.

Once inside his study, Daniel groaned audibly as he seated himself behind the old oak desk. Remorse and righteous indignation pinballed him around. He was profoundly shaken. Never had he spoken to Carole in such a manner. But now as he relived flashbacks of their conversation, he realized that the real revelation had been made to himself! And when he looked into the mirror of his soul, he wanted to weep.

His instincts led him to believe he was right about Carole's obsession with Tim. But his mouth had put him in the one position he had always tried to avoid at all costs—a win-lose situation. One of the things Daniel practiced like a politician was the fine art of diplomacy. He had learned to handle crisis with tact, never putting either himself or the other person in a position where one party won and the other lost. He prided himself on his uncompromising stand on the Gospel, but when working with people, he had a gift for arriving at a solution that usually satisfied everyone. Now he had taken a rock-like stand with his own wife. "Don't make me wait too long."

The veiled threat rang in his ears. Had he really said that? Had he pushed her too far? Once before, she had run from him when things got too much for her, and he'd spent harrowing days trying to find her. He shivered at the possibility of replaying that scene.

There is no way we can go back to the days before Tim was born, he conceded. *But something has to change.* He struck the desk with his fist. *But why did you have to be so blunt?* he chastized himself. *You've counseled so many other couples, helped them work out their problems. Surely you could have done better that that!*

He leaned back in his chair and closed his eyes. The urge to call Carole to apologize swelled in him. He eyed the phone. *What would you say? Sorry, I was wrong? I wasn't. Sorry I mentioned it? Maybe.* He didn't believe he was wrong, but he was tired of feeling like an extra appendage in Carole's life. *Still, I should have been more tactful.*

His call packet lay on the desk. *What should I do, Lord?* For a split second he wanted to accept the call and start all over. *By yourself, old man? Now who's running away?*

Life was crowding in on Daniel. The list of visits he needed to make were piling up daily. The fall stewardship program was getting off to a slow start. He'd had a critical letter, accusing him of everything but adultery—anonymous, of course.

He honestly didn't know what to do about his call to St. Paul's. He suspected Carole was not ready to move. Sermon-writing was getting increasingly difficult, and his adult Bible class had recently acquired a new member who argued with Daniel's every theological statement. And now the core that had helped make all these problems bearable was crumbling around him.

With surprising honesty he realized that he didn't want to go home after work. Home was an uncomfortable place right now. *I definitely feel unloved and over-burdened today. Dear Lord, hold me up, for I'm faltering under this load. Send the Comforter, and ease my sadness.* The anger drained away, leaving him incredibly fatigued.

When the phone rang, he grabbed it, hoping to hear Carole's voice. It was Susan Lapney's.

"Pastor, could you come over right away? I need to talk with you privately."

She sounded upset. "Why, of course. I can be at your house in about fifteen minutes. Are you all right?"

"Yes, but I need to see you."

As she hung up, he mentally slipped into his shepherd's role. *Probably trouble with Al,* he reasoned. It was easy to put aside his own problems. Someone needed him.

At the first knock, Susan opened the door and invited Daniel in. She appeared nervous as she led him into the kitchen and served him coffee at her kitchen table.

Daniel made small talk until she was ready to confide in him. But they were on their second cup of coffee before she managed to tell him the reason for her mysterious phone call.

"You can't take that call to St. Paul's. I just couldn't bear it." Susan regarded him steadily, rushing on before Daniel could reply. "I'm in love with you, and I'd die if you left. You're my whole world."

Daniel's cup hovered in mid-air, the desire to laugh dangerously strong. He opened his mouth to acknowledge her ridiculous declaration, but the words were stuck behind the laugh.

"Wait, don't say anything. Just let me get this all out." Calmly and unashamedly, she poured out her heart. "I've loved you from the first minute I saw you in the pulpit. You were everything I've ever wanted in a man." She rose and came to kneel at his feet, gazing up into his face with huge brown eyes.

Daniel was thunderstruck.

"Don't be afraid of me," Susan spoke reassuringly. "I won't make trouble for you. Al is gone, will be for hours. We're here alone." She bent her head and rested it against his knee, sighing. "I've dreamed so often of this moment."

A protest finally bubbled up out of Daniel's mouth. "Susan, *no*." Looking down, he realized for the first time how provocatively she was dressed and raised his eyes. As vulnerable as she was, though, he dared not humiliate her. It would be the cruelest thing he could do.

Awkwardly he tried to rise, but Susan stood first. Looking down at him, she tried to soothe his fears. "I've surprised you, haven't I? I assumed you knew. We spend so much time together, I thought you'd have guessed by now."

The sun slanting in from the window behind her illuminated her small, attractive body, and Daniel was keenly aware of her nearness. When he finally gained his feet, Susan moved to nestle against him, her arms wrapped around his waist.

"Oh, you smell so good," she breathed. "Al rarely does. But you're always so beautifully groomed."

Daniel stood there dumbly, sensing a spider's web being spun seductively around him. But her next words broke his immobility.

"Kiss me," she said softly, tilting her head.

Firmly he pushed her away, his hands on her shoulders. Holding her at arm's length, Daniel spoke to her as one speaks to a child—very gently, very kindly. "Susan, look at me. You're a fine woman...with a husband. And I am deeply in love with my wife. This is wrong for both of us."

"Oh, don't tell me you're flattered by my 'crush' and all that garbage!" She was so sure of herself. "I do love you. You're so...so pure. So close to God. I feel better just loving you. You make my whole life worthwhile."

Daniel dropped his hands from her shoulders and moved to the kitchen cabinet, leaving her standing by the table. "You know that this could only tear both our families apart. It would destroy all of us. I could never let that happen, of course. But I want you to know that I love you, too, but I love you as a dear, trusted *friend*. Nothing must violate that trust. Do you understand?"

Tears glistened in Susan's eyes. He hoped he saw the pain of acceptance there, too. "Yes I—I understand. But *nothing* will change the way I feel about you."

"I've got to go." What now? Thank you for the coffee? Daniel felt like a marathon runner who had hit the wall after too many miles of endless running. He must not encourage her, and yet he mustn't hurt her either. "Thank you for sharing your secret with me, Susan. I'll always . . . remember." That was certainly no lie!

Susan was reluctant to let him go. "I won't make trouble for you, I promise. Just don't leave Longview. You're all I have to keep me going. Let me at least see you, hear your voice, love you from a distance—"

Distance was what Daniel had in mind. The more the better. "I haven't made a decision on my call yet. Please, think seriously about what I've told you about Carole and Al. Goodbye, Susan."

He walked deliberately out of the room, stifling the impulse to run. Home to Carole. Home to safety. He never looked back. And as he drove, the story of Joseph and Potiphar's wife skittered through his mind.

Joseph had fled, too, but Potiphar's wife had accused him of a crime for spite. Would Susan do the same thing? "How can I do this great wickedness and sin against God?" Joseph had asked. Daniel wasn't even tempted to commit the "wickedness." And yet Susan could ruin his entire life with a few words.

Daniel was several blocks away before he realized he was holding his breath, and quickly sucked in deep gulps of air. Slowly the tension and shock began to ease.

Only an hour ago he'd been sitting in his study, feeling sorry for himself. *I was feeling so unloved. Lord, save me from myself.*

Carole could hear Tim beginning to fret in the nursery after his morning nap.

"I'm coming," she called as she hurried down the hallway. "You *do* have me on a short leash, don't you, young man?" she scolded as she lifted him from his crib.

Swiftly changing the hungry child, she settled down in the rocker to feed him. "Your father will be home for lunch at noon. He expects to be fed, too, you know." In his greediness, Tim completely ignored her soft reminder. "We really have to change some things around here, little one. I love you dearly, but your father has his rights, too. And," she added, "he made that quite clear this morning."

A flash of anger accompanied the memory of Daniel's

threat. How long was "too long"? It frightened her to think of the possible consequences. She had never seen him so angry at her.

Her fingers played lightly with the fine baby hair that wisped on Tim's forehead. "After you eat, I'll take you in the kitchen with me, and we'll get a nice lunch together for your dad." His chubby little arms and legs wriggled in pleasure at the sound of her voice.

Anguish twisted her heart, and she blinked back tears. "How can I go away and leave you? You're only seven weeks old, and I'm the only one who really knows what you need. Besides, you're *my* responsibility, not some baby-sitter's."

Carole resented Daniel's stubborn stance, putting her in the position of choosing. As much as she loved her husband, his needs were not as critical as Tim's. She knew she must tell Daniel she couldn't go with him on the trip, comforting herself with the thought that this time, he'd asked too much of her.

He's being completely unreasonable, she decided. Now all that remained was to tell him so. And the sooner, the better.

Carefully she prepared an especially delicious lunch, and waited for Daniel to come home. *At least he can't say I don't take good care of him,* she thought with satisfaction, surveying the attractive table.

As the hands of the clock sped by, her anxiety mounted. She was doing laundry when the outside door into the utility room finally opened. Remembering Daniel's angry ultimatum earlier in the day, she waited for a signal from him.

"Hi." He leaned over and kissed her on the mouth.

"Hi." He didn't appear angry, only guarded. *He's waiting to see if I'm going to bring up the trip.*

Carole felt caught between submitting to what she considered an unreasonable demand, and trying to please the man she loved. A sudden stab of fear clutched her heart. For the first time, divided in their goals, she saw a faint crack appear in the secure wall around their marriage. If neither of them acquiesced, what would happen? She put down the clothes and followed him into the kitchen.

"Your lunch is ready." A tiny olive branch in the midst of the storm.

Daniel was washing his hands in the kitchen sink. He carefully dried them on a paper towel and sat down at the cheerful table. He didn't seem to notice the bright yellow tablecloth.

He's still angry, Carole decided. *Careful now. Careful.* Like a doe with a fawn at the edge of the forest, sniffing a suspicious scent, she began putting the food on the table.

Daniel spoke first. "Is Tim asleep?"

"Yes, I fed him cereal for the first time today. He wasn't crazy about it, but he ate it." With horror, Carole realized she was talking about the baby again. She ducked her head and tried to regroup.

"Cereal, huh?" Daniel picked up on the theme. "He's getting to be a big boy. Hey, *this* looks good." He turned his attention to the food she was putting before him.

To Carole, everything seemed so superficial. They were talking, but certainly not communicating. Safe, but disturbing. For the first time in their marriage, they were tiptoeing arond something large and dark and hurtful. Something neither of them was ready to address.

"Anything interesting happen at the office today?"

There, she was showing concern for his life. Then an expression she didn't recognize flitted across Daniel's face.

"No, just the usual. Rhoda wasn't there and I had the place to myself." He took a large bite of his sandwich.

Something was wrong. What was that look she had seen so fleetingly? Fear? No, not fear. Her skin prickled as she identified the look. Perhaps *lying* was too strong. *Evasive* seemed more accurate. He wasn't telling her something. And she had no right to ask him about it. But something had happened at the office today that he wouldn't, or couldn't, tell her.

Remembering her years of training, she resisted the urge to question him further. There were many things that happened in the course of a minister's day that he was not allowed to share with her. Confidential counseling sessions. Professional secrets. Afraid of saying something to make things worse between then, she fell silent.

"This is good." Daniel took another bite, the food in his mouth excusing him from further conversation.

"Thank you." Carole picked at her food, wondering what to say. Never had the well of conversation run so dry.

When Tim cried, she was glad for the reprieve. Silently she went into the nursery and sat down in the rocker to nurse him. A scalding wall of tears built up behind her eyes, but she made a concentrated effort to hold them back. She was totally miserable.

A tiny reflex of fear pinged down her body when she heard Daniel's soft footsteps on the hall carpet, heading her way.

He paused, standing tall in the doorway of the room. "Is he asleep yet?"

"Soon."

He nodded his head and turned away, moving into their bedroom. She heard the French doors click open. He was going out in their private garden just off the room.

She laid her sleeping son back in his crib and tried to decide what to do next. If she followed Daniel, he was sure to expect an answer about the trip. No matter what she chose, it would be the wrong choice.

Desperately she wished for a friend in whom to confide, realizing that Joyce was too far removed from her life presently to understand. Her sister would immediately take Daniel's side. And her very best friend was out in the garden, a million miles away from her. She rocked herself in the chair, seeking the consolation she gave so easily to Tim each day.

There was only One who could help her, and she turned to Him now. "Lord," she whispered, "I'm in real trouble. You know the problem and you know how I feel. What should I do? Is Daniel right?"

There were no flashes of lightning, no visions, no voices. But there was a sense of peace that flooded her. She had placed her problem in wise and capable hands.

Slowly she rose and followed Daniel out into the garden. He was standing in the shade, oblivious to the heavy flowery smells. Her heart reached out for him, loving him, and yet a little frightened of the intensity of his feelings.

He heard her footsteps and turned, enfolding her in his arms, pulling her close against his broad chest. She allowed him to pour out his love to her wordlessly. He kissed the top of her shining hair, pressed his lips against her forehead. At this moment, nothing and no one else existed.

His mouth slid close to her ear. "I love you, Carole, and I'm sorry about this morning."

"No, no—" She placed soft fingers over his lips—"you were right." She lifted her head to look up at him. "I'll go with you on the trip. How could I refuse you anything?"

The radiance of his smile took her breath.

"But I can't leave Tim," she added flatly, "so I guess you're stuck with the two of us." Would he be angry again?

She was more than a little surprised by his reply. "Don't worry. Everything will work out. You'll see."

ten

The highway stretching out in front of them shimmered in the mid-morning heat, forming mirages which retreated and re-formed, always just out of reach. The heat also hugged the vegetation like Spanish moss, sucking the moisture out a little at a time. Pine and oak trees held out their branches as if in supplication for relief. And the grass was beginning to turn brown, giving the scant pastureland a quilt-like effect.

Fortunately, the air conditioner made the car a moving refuge from the cloying humidity.

Tim slept peacefully in his carrier in the back seat, giving Daniel and Carole long periods of time to talk without interruption. They exchanged glances, and Daniel reached out to take her hand.

"Happy?"

"Very." She returned his smile. "I feel as though we're on vacation."

He nodded, content with his lot. Even though he was on a serious mission, for the moment he was relieved of all responsibility and was feeling playful and cheerful, ready for adventure with his best girl beside him. And his son. Secretly he had been afraid that traveling with Tim might present a major problem, but so far the baby had slept most of the time. And when he was awake, he had provided his parents with delightful company. *Thank you, Lord,* Daniel breathed gratefully.

The city they entered was like a thousand other cities in Texas—shopping malls, grocery stores, and gas stations. The only thing that set it apart was the fact that maybe, just maybe, they would be living here in the next few months.

They checked into a large motel with a distinctly Spanish flavor—white stucco with red-tiled roof.

Once they were settled, Daniel reached for the phone. "Better let someone know we're here."

Carole unpacked while he phoned the interim pastor, John Hallman.

"The Hallmans are going to take us to dinner," Daniel reported when he hung up. "He said there's a terrific place called Szechuan Gardens." Daniel stuck out his lower lip in a pout. "I'm not going to have to use chopsticks again, am I?"

Carole laughed at the silly face he made. "Maybe it's some kind of test. If you can't use chopsticks, you won't fit in here."

"But this is Texas," he protested. "Why is everyone so hung up on Chinese food? What ever happened to steak or barbecue?"

"Come on, my gourmet husband, get your shower while I take care of Tim."

He gave her a sly look. "In the interest of conservation of our environment, we could save water if we showered together."

"Oh, you're a clever one." She kissed him lightly, skillfully maneuvering out of his grasp. "Dinner. The Hallmans. Remember?"

Daniel had been looking forward to this trip as a special time of R & R for the two of them—Romance and Renewal. *Maybe later*, he hoped.

The Hallmans were a likable couple, whom Daniel calculated to be about their age. It was only moments before Bethany Hallman had Tim's rapt attention.

"My wife has never met a baby she didn't like," John Hallman explained with an indulgent grin at his wife.

"That's why I'm a pediatric nurse, dear," she shot back before turning to Carole and Daniel. "And soon we'll have a child of our own. We're adopting, and the mother is due next month."

"You must be thrilled," Carole said, feeling instant rapport with the attractive brunette.

"Get ready for some major changes in your life," Daniel warned with a laugh, then quickly changed the subject.

At the restaurant the two couples exchanged information about families and churches. Daniel was impressed with John's sales pitch on the town of Stephenville. But when he asked about the church, his new friend was evasive.

"I'll give you all the information you want after you've met with the council," John told him. "I just don't want you to form your impression of St. Paul's based on anything I have to say. You need to see for yourself. I can only assure you they're fine people and eager to meet both of you." Taking off his horn-rimmed glasses, John polished the lenses with a handkerchief. "Once when I visited a church, the pastor there gave me a real razzle-dazzle buildup. All I can say is, the guy must have been a used car salesman before he went into the ministry. I promised myself then and there I'd never do that to someone else."

Daniel appreciated the man's honesty and forthrightness, and said so.

After dinner, with Daniel still commenting on the good food, they drove to the church to meet with the council.

In the darkness it was hard to make out the contours of the church building, but it seemed to follow the lines of traditional architecture. And Daniel was pleased to note the well-kept grounds. That was always a good sign.

The meeting was an informal one. There was the ever-present coffee, cold drinks, and desserts laid out attractively on a table centered with a flower arrangement. John introduced them to a group of about twenty men and women, and they visited for a few minutes before the meeting officially began.

It was easy for Daniel to pick out the president of the congregation. He was a definite leader among them and seemed to command their respect. It was with this man Daniel hoped to spend time.

The balance of people on the council—an equal number of men and women—was another indication of the temper of the congregation. The Sunday school superintendent was a woman, sharp and well educated. All in all he was impressed with the caliber of the membership. But he was aware that he was also being scrutinized, just as he was measuring them.

Daniel glanced over to the side, where Carole was standing with Bethany and Tim. They had gathered a small crowd. Bethany had not relinquished her hold on the baby, and Daniel could tell that Carole was relaxed and enjoying herself.

The meeting ended on a pleasant note, and the two told the Hallmans good night at the entrance to the motel, promising to join the couple for dinner at their house the following evening.

When they returned to their room, Carole changed Tim and got him ready for bed. Daniel watched her graceful movements as she performed her motherly tasks. While she nursed the baby once more, they talked over their first impressions of the church and the people they had met.

But Daniel's mind wasn't on the conversation. "Do you remember the last time we stayed in a motel?"

"It wasn't a motel, it was a very fancy hotel," she corrected him. "The Fairmont in Dallas, when we went to the convention before we were married." Her eyes sparked with laughter at the memory.

"'Before we were married,' is the operative phrase."

Carole had just finished nursing Tim and was putting him in his crib when Daniel walked up to her and pulled her close. "That trip represented one of my more heroic efforts in self-control."

"Well, we're married *now*," Carole teased softly.

And when at last Daniel fell asleep, her name was on his lips.

They spent the next day in unhurried activity. John came by to drive them around the area and give them an opportunity to get a feel for the town that might be their new home.

Despite the relaxed environment, Carole felt a certain tension. She really didn't want to leave her home, her friends, the familiar routine. On the other hand, of course, she could do whatever she had to do, whatever Daniel felt was right. But when she tried to read his face, she didn't have a clue as to his intentions.

She and Tim slept the afternoon away, while Daniel swam and read by the pool. And when she awoke, it was time to dress for dinner.

Although the casual affair at the Hallmans' home was a social event, there was an underlying air of serious business that Carole didn't fail to detect.

"Daniel," John began, soon after the meal was over, "I'm not unaware that you seem very happy with your present situation, so we appreciate your coming all this way to meet with the council." He grinned. "You and your family made quite a hit last night. One of the men told me to put some muscle on you to get you here."

Daniel's laugh was pleasant, but noncommittal. "Thanks for the warning, John."

"With your track record, I'm sure you'd do a super job here. And Carole, with her poise and talent, would definitely be an asset."

Carole blushed slightly. "Are you Irish, John? Between your red hair and your blarney, I'm not sure what to believe."

Bethany spoke up. "Oh, he's a smoothie, all right, but I agree with him one hundred percent. It would be great to have you close by, so our children could play together."

The men fell into conversation about the meeting, and Bethany took Carole aside to share more intimately. "I don't know what to do about my job. They're so short-handed at the hospital I hate to quit, but I can't stand the thought of finally having a baby and then not being able to take care of him myself. Do you work outside the home, Carole?"

"I *did*. I was an on-staff counselor at the bank." Carole glanced at Daniel. "I suppose we need to discuss it someday soon. To tell you the truth, I don't know whether to go back or not. Of course, as long as I'm nursing Tim,

I *can't*." She looked again at her husband. "It would cause all sorts of new problems if I did go back to work. But to be honest, sometimes I miss all the excitement of dealing with other people's problems. Being a full-time mom has definitely taken all my time."

"Millions of mothers work because they have no other choice," John broke in, overhearing her last remark.

"I wonder what effect the working mother will have on children?" Daniel interjected, leading Carole to suspect that he'd already been giving the matter some thought. "Does it harm them, or make them better able to cope with life?"

John smiled. "Depends on which book you read."

"I really loved my job," Carole said a little hesitantly, still not sure how Daniel felt about it. "There were so many challenges, and I think I was good at it."

"You were quite good at it," Daniel confirmed. "But I think I'm glad you're at home with Tim right now. There's plenty of time to think about going back to work. Maybe after he starts to school."

"But then there's the room mother stuff and school plays. Who would be there for all that?" Carole knew there was much to consider.

"The issue of working mothers is a problem for which there seems to be no good answer," concluded John. "I do know that the dual role causes a great deal of stress in a marriage. Many of the couples I counsel find it's their core problem. The wife resents the fact that her husband won't help with the household chores. He feels he shouldn't have to. The husband doesn't feel he should have to work all day in the office and then come home to housework, too. Or sometimes he's just locked into his culture. It isn't the 'manly' thing to do."

"Or sometimes it's the *wife's* problem," Bethany pitched in. "Hassling her husband about helping around the house is more trouble than it's worth. And some women don't *want* their husbands' help. *Voila.* Supermom." Bethany looked thoughtful. "I wonder if that will be my trouble."

"Probably," John teased. "You always did take on the problems of the world."

At that, Bethany offered more coffee. And Daniel found himself somewhat relieved that the discussion had come to an end. It was too complicated a problem to be conversation for an evening's entertainment. In fact, he'd wrestled with it in counseling sessions on more than one occasion. Now it appeared that he and Carole had their work cut out for them.

Actually, until tonight, he hadn't realized that she had been considered going back to the bank. She'd always spoken of her job in only the most casual terms. Now she seemed intent on broadening her horizons, and he wondered if his own remarks about her over-absorption with Tim had provided the catalyst. Had he opened a Pandora's box in his own life?

What *did* a woman do with her time after her children were in school? He was reminded of one woman who spent her time living in a fantasy world. A world built around *him*. Hurriedly he pushed that thought away. At least that was one problem solved.

The conversation finally divided the couples once more, with the men talking churches and Daniel's call to Stephenville, and Carole and Bethany talking babies and jobs. Carole spoke lovingly of Leigh and the course their lives seemed to be taking. All in all it was a very satisfying evening.

On their way back to the motel, Daniel and Carole commented fondly on their new friends, the Hallmans. All four had bonded quickly and the fledgling relationship already felt comfortable, as if they had known each other always.

When Daniel brought up the question of how to spend their last day in the area, Carole had an idea. "I'd hoped we might go into Dallas. It would be a shame to miss Big D when we're so close."

"How about shopping at the Galleria?"

Carole blew him a kiss. That settled, their conversation turned to the important decision facing Daniel. "I'll be seeing the president of the congregation in the morning before we leave for Dallas, Carole. What do you think? Is this a serious call?"

"Well, I should think there would have to be some heavy-duty prayer before you'll know the answer to that."

"But how would you like living here?"

She was vague. "It seems like a nice place. The people at the church were certainly nice."

Daniel gave her a sidelong glance. "You used the word *nice* twice. *Nice* is a tepid word. Neither hot nor cold."

He fell silent, realizing how accurately he had called it. Carole certainly didn't share his enthusiasm for this place as a possible parish. *She's neither hot nor cold. OK, Lord, what do I do now?*

eleven

Rolling ranch land gave way to sprawling suburban neighborhoods on their approach to the city the next morning. In the misty distance Carole could see the blurred monoliths that marked downtown Dallas. Traffic was heavy because of repairs on the Expressway, but urban drivers were amazingly well-mannered, politely taking turns as the lanes narrowed.

Carole's heart always seemed to beat a little faster in Dallas. The tempo of the city was exhilarating, and once again she was briefly tempted to return to the stimulating environment of the workplace, where *all* her gifts could be exercised. *On the other hand,* she thought pragmatically, *if I were working, I couldn't be here!* She intended to enjoy every moment of this adventure.

In spite of the Galleria's spacious interior design, the place was packed with people, the very atmosphere charged with excitement. Fountains splashed playfully in the glassed-in central atrium, and tall palms seemed to be reaching for the sun. Carefully tended flower beds were artfully tucked beside benches to entice weary shoppers. But the center of the building was devoted to a sunken skating rink, where shoppers could watch people gliding over the glazed surface, even in the hottest of the summer months.

"Oh, Daniel!" Carole gasped with pleasure. "I love coming here. It gives me such *energy.*"

Daniel was dubious. "It gives *me* a pain. There are too many shops for any one human to take in, especially a reluctant male." Then, at the sight of her glowing face, he relented. "But I'm glad we're here."

They picked up a stroller for Tim and window-shopped their way to a teen boutique.

Daniel saw the telltale look in Carole's eyes before she spoke. "I think I'm about to make a purchase." He tried to look forlorn, but it was wasted motion. His wife was already inside the store, browsing through a rack of blouses.

"Look at this, Daniel! It's perfect for Leigh."

"If you select it, I'm sure she'll love it." He watched as she singled out a skirt to go with the blouse, then marched up to the counter where she stood looking at him expectantly.

"I guess this is where I come in," he said, pulling out his wallet.

"Thank you, darling. You're a generous man." The cost of the garments had come as a surprise to both of them. Keeping a teenager fashionably dressed was an expensive proposition.

And clothing was only a small part of the high cost of bringing up children. There would be school supplies. Medical expenses. Entertainment. Graduation. Cars. Insurance. College for Leigh in the fall. Carole felt her stomach tighten at the thought of the financial obligations looming ahead. Suddenly her old job seemed more than a selfish whim. She and Daniel must have a serious talk soon.

Each shop window was an opportunity for Carole to see a reflection of their little family. She had let her hair down—literally—for this trip. It fell, shining and free, around her shoulders. She was dressed comfortably in a pale blue cotton shirt and denim skirt and wore strappy little gold sandals on her bare feet. Her tall husband, pushing Tim's stroller beside her, looked every inch the casual executive.

All in all they appeared to be the image of today's young family. The anonymity pleased her greatly. No one knew or cared who they were. Pastor and Mrs. Thornton could move, unnoticed, through the crowd.

Carole still wrestled now and then with her true identity, chafing under the label—"the Pastor's wife"—imposed by Daniel's role. She had become quite adept at reminding herself frequently that she was still Carole Morgan, a person in her own right.

They shopped the morning away, stopping for shish-kabobs, rice, and a Greek salad filled with very salty Greek olives, after which Carole and Tim made a rest stop.

The ladies' lounge was tastefully appointed, with a baby changing table and a couch where Carole could nurse Tim. Again she marveled at the assistance afforded young mothers away from home.

Rejoining Daniel, Carole and Tim strolled along beside him, unaware that her husband was steering them toward a jewelry store.

Looking at the sign in the window, she frowned. "There's no reason to stop here. I've done all the shopping I'd planned to do."

"Oh, I think you'll reconsider when you see what I have in mind." He led her over to a counter where a salesman was displaying a gold chain, a modest diamond sparkling in its filigreed setting. "For you. Something to remember

Stephenville by."

Carole was stunned. "Daniel Thornton! Just about the time I think there are no more surprises, you prove me wrong!" Over her protests, he fastened the pendant around her neck. "Thank you, darling," she whispered. "This is good for at least a dozen chicken-fried steak dinners. And it will always remind me of this special trip. . .and the dearest husband any woman ever had." The blaze of love in her eyes rivaled the diamond's brilliance.

In the soft haze of early evening, the sun-beaten landscape flashed past them on the way back to Longview.

"No matter how much I enjoy getting away," Daniel began, setting the cruise control on the car, "going home is always the best part of a trip."

"Hmmm." With Tim napping in the back, Carole was too mellow to do more than murmur a response. Laying her head against the back of the seat, she closed her eyes and relived portions of the past three days—meeting the members of St. Paul's, becoming friends with the Hallmans, shopping at the Galleria. But most amazing of all had been the baby's adaptability to his new environment. Tim had been a dream!

What had made things so different on the road? Carole wracked her brain. For one thing, she herself had experienced almost no conflict of interest where Daniel and Tim were concerned. Why? Could it have been because their world away from home was so small—just the three of them, with no outside distractions? Was it because Daniel had been there to observe everything that went on, to help when Tim needed something? Had that made him feel more a part of things, less of an intruder? She shook her head, confused. Whatever the reason, the entire trip had been a peaceful event.

It had also been a revealing one. Faced with some stark financial realities, even if they moved to the larger church, Carole knew that the needs of their growing family might now require two paychecks. She fingered the expensive pendant around her neck, feeling a little guilty, but there was no way she would give it back. It was a love gift from Daniel. Privately she felt he shouldn't be spending this money on her, but she loved him for it.

Money. Could she get her old job back if they stayed in Longview? The bank had agreed to hold it for her for two months. That time had just run out.

"Penny for your thoughts," Daniel said, looking over to be sure she was awake.

"I was thinking what a fantastic trip this has been," she said, half-truthfully." Soberly she added, "You were right to insist that I go with you."

"I'm glad it worked out the way it did, otherwise I think I might be a bachelor today."

She glanced at him without comment. Beneath the lighthearted banter was the frightening ring of truth. She knew they had been locked in some sort of struggle, one that could have shattered their marriage if they hadn't taken measures to change things between them. She suspected that Daniel, too, was hoping the changes would be lasting.

He reached over to take her hand. "Things will be better when we get home, I promise."

Lifting her hand to his lips, he sealed the promise with a kiss on her soft fingertips. Their eyes met briefly before he turned to watch the road again.

"Daniel," she began hesitantly, "we need to talk...about the possibility of my going back to work."

His countenance was grave. "After the conversation with the Hallmans, I should think that would be the *last* thing you would seriously consider."

"I've learned some things on this trip, darling, that we simply have to face. For example, I never dreamed it would cost so much to clothe a teenager...and with a baby, too...well, the next few years will be expensive, to say the least." She hurried on before he had a chance to reply. "I know you make a good salary, and we have a small savings account, but they're *my* children, too, and I'd like to help. Besides, you're the one who said that since Tim came, my world has become too narrow."

Daniel grimaced. Was he going to be hanged by his own words? He tried the practical approach. "Yes, but who would take care of him? That would be quite an expense, too. And you'd need clothes for the office."

"I know we couldn't expect Pearl to take on the extra responsibility for Tim for nothing, but I won't be needing any more new clothes for a while," Carole assured him. "Some of my old things weren't worn much before I got pregnant with Tim. Remember?"

"I remember."

The terse reply and the way he tensed his jaw were sure signs he was annoyed, and Carole attempted to bridge the widening gap between them. "I didn't mean to start a fight on the way home from our glorious trip, especially since we just promised things would be different."

"I didn't mean *that* different," he retorted.

"Well, darling, I'm not even sure I can get my job back," she said soothingly. "They may have filled it already. But, if I could, I think I'd like to give it a try." She paused. "I was good at it, you said so yourself."

"But what if I decide to take the call to Stephenville? That's a real possibility, you know."

"Let's cross that bridge when we get to it. In fact, if I don't get the job, maybe that could be a sign that you are to accept the call," she finished triumphantly.

They had always operated on the premise that God works daily in the lives of His children and provides clear roadmarks as to which direction to take.

"All right, give it a try," he agreed reluctantly. "But maybe you could work only part time, not full time. That would make a major difference."

It was a reasonable compromise.

"Good idea, darling! Maybe I could ask about working Mondays, Wednesdays, and Fridays, on an appointment basis." The idea was appealing, and she glanced at Daniel gratefully. "Thanks for giving me a chance."

He didn't reply and she let the subject drop. At least, he had given her his blessing, sort of. Now it was up to her to make it work. . .for *all* of them.

Daniel came first, of course. Silently she vowed that somehow she would keep her husband happy.

Carole's hand was trembling on the receiver the next morning as she waited to speak with the personnel director at the bank. As she waited she thought back over the events of the past few hours. The homecoming had been warm and satisfying, with Leigh delighted to have them back and overjoyed with her gifts. Carole felt another step closer in her relationship with her stepdaughter.

When her former employer came on the line, he seemed

pleased to hear from her and assured her that they had not yet filled her position. "I had a feeling you'd want to come back. I couldn't imagine you as a housewife for very long."

Carole wasn't quite sure that was a compliment, but outlined her request for a work schedule.

"I don't see why that wouldn't work," Mr. Pitner said. "Let's at least give it a try. Want to start this week?"

She was startled by his swift acceptance of her offer. "Well, I'll have to get my baby-sitter lined up, but I think I can take care of that by next Monday."

"We'll have to make some salary adjustments," he went on, "but I expect this arrangement to be mutually beneficial. We've certainly missed you around here."

This time Carole recognized the compliment and couldn't contain a sudden rush of joy. "Thank you. See you Monday morning, bright and early." She was still smiling as she hung up the phone.

The smile faded a bit, however, when she talked to Daniel. "I'll miss not having you around on my day off," was his initial reaction.

She was disappointed. Even though he had agreed to her work schedule, obviously he had hoped it wouldn't work out.

"I'm happy about this, Daniel," she said evenly. "Please try to be happy for me."

But his businesslike tone was more formal than friendly. "Now that we know what we're dealing with, we'll need to sit down and work out the logistics."

Eager to avoid an unpleasant scene over the phone, Carole quickly agreed. "Of course. We can do that at supper if you like."

As soon as she had finished talking to Daniel, she called Pearl, but was unprepared for the woman's negative response to her news. "I sure do hate to hear that you're going to be a working mother. Tim needs you right now. What are you going to do about nursing him?"

That annoyed Carole. As if she hadn't thought all that through! "I have a week to wean him to the bottle," she explained, hating herself for feeling defensive. "I can still nurse him on the days I'm not working."

"You know I would never turn you down. If *you're* not going to be around, then he needs *someone* who knows him really well." Carole cringed at the implied rebuke. "But I warn you, you'll miss out on some of the best parts. Won't be too long 'til the little fellow starts crawling, and then he'll be walking. I think he may have already started to cut a tooth. He was chewing like crazy when I had him last." There was another significant pause. "But you do what you have to do. I'll be glad to help you out."

They agreed on a salary, and Carole hung up with new doubts assailing her. Pearl was right. She would miss out on some of the milestones in Tim's young life. *But I won't be gone every day,* she argued to herself. *And I know I can make this work.*

At supper Daniel presented a long list of adjustments he felt would have to be made. On the days Pearl came to keep Tim, she could cook dinner. Carole made a mental note to plan menus and keep the pantry well stocked.

Then there would be the problem of getting Leigh to and from classes when they started in a few weeks. Ultimately it was decided that Carole would deliver Leigh on her way to work and Daniel would pick her up in the afternoons. And some of those days, she could carpool with Georgianna.

Failing to think of any other potential hindrances to their new routine, they left the table, satisfied the household would run smoothly.

This is going to work! It's really going to work! Carole told herself the night before she was to report to the bank. The meal-planning had been carefully thought out, the groceries put away. Leigh, of course, would not be starting to school for a while yet, so she would be a backup for Pearl. Carole had selected a tailored summer suit for her first day back, and had washed her hair. Now, despite all obstacles, she was as excited as a child on her first day of school.

At ten o'clock she perched on the edge of the bed and set the alarm clock for six. Turning to Daniel, who was propped up in bed reading a magazine, she said firmly, "Good night, darling. Big day tomorrow," and crawled into her side.

Even after the light was out, Carole stayed awake, long past the time she had intended to be asleep. But she was too preoccupied with her own plans to notice that Daniel's back, turned to her, was decidedly rigid.

twelve

"Seven o'clock!" Carole cracked one bleary eye to read the digital clock. "Why didn't the alarm go off?" She lunged out of bed in a panic, then comforted herself with the knowledge that she was prepared to meet the day.

Eager to make up the lost time, she hopped into the shower, careful not to get her hair wet, then applied makeup at the bathroom mirror. In the kitchen she grabbed a quick cup of coffee and put two slices of whole wheat bread in the toaster. *So far, so good.*

Tim, however, was another matter. He fought the bottle she offered him, and sensing her anxiety, fretted while she juggled his feeding and her own breakfast of dry toast. "Oh, no, Tim, not today! Please!" She put him back in his crib, where he continued to fuss the whole time she was dressing.

Daniel slept through it all. She watched him as she hurried into her clothes, thinking unkindly, *Why couldn't you have gotten up to help me the first day?*

She was relieved when Pearl bustled in, after using her own key. "Am I glad to see you!"

The kindly woman picked up the unhappy baby, and Carole was able to finish putting her hair up in a neat chignon. With an eye on the clock, she made a last-minute check of her appearance. Everything seemed to be in the right place, and her jangled nerves relaxed a bit.

It was at that moment that Daniel's alarm went off right beside her, shrilling through the quiet room. She grabbed her chest and let out a small shriek.

At her startled cry, Daniel's eyes flew open. "A little jumpy this morning, aren't you, love?"

"I don't even have time to tell you more than. . .thanks for the help on this horrendous morning." Her reply was dripping with sarcasm.

"Hey, this is my day off, remember?" he defended himself.

She gave him an icy stare, then shrugged. "Never mind. I've got to go or I'll be late."

"If it helps any, you look very nice." Perhaps his smile was genuine, but Carole wondered if he was a little smug about her day starting badly. "Have a nice day at the office, dear," he said sweetly.

"Bye." She leaned over to give him a peck on the cheek and was out the door.

On her way, she kissed Tim and waved at Pearl.

Carole was relieved when she was in the car at last. But when she tried to start the engine, it only coughed and sputtered impotently. She tried again. . .and again. "Please, Lord, make it start," she whispered frantically.

Hearing her futile attempts, Daniel stuck his head out of the utility door into the garage. "Scoot over and let me try." He turned the key and the motor fired up immediately. "Don't let it die. I'll check it for you tonight when you get home." Daniel's smile was dangerously close to a smirk as he closed the car door and waved her off.

If she hadn't been such a wreck by this time, Carole would have made some caustic remark about her mechanic's appearance. Daniel's hair was standing straight up in back and he was still in his rumpled pajamas. Instead, she silently thanked the Lord that the car was at last running smoothly, even if it had cost her a piece of her pride.

She tried deep breathing to regain her composure as she drove through the heavy morning traffic, but her eyes were continually darting to the accusing clock on the dashboard. "I haven't been this much of a slave to the clock in months," she muttered. "Lord, is this Your way of telling me I should stay home with Tim?"

There was no immediate answer, but He did grant her a parking space near the front door of the bank. "Thank You, Lord," she breathed. "You knew I didn't want to be late on my very first day." She breezed through the door a minute after eight.

Mr. Pitner, her old boss, greeted her at her office door. "Good to have you back, Carole. I see you're as prompt as ever." He quirked a brow at her sudden burst of laughter. "Nervous mother syndrome?"

"Does it get better?"

"My wife says so." He grinned. "Of course, there are those occasional days when she threatens to sail off to Tahiti alone. Just hang in there, and...have a better day," he threw over his shoulder as he hurried off.

She smiled at his retreating back and went into her office, then took a few deep breaths and put the unfortunate beginning behind her.

On her desk were files of clients who would be coming in to see her today, and she took a moment to reacquaint herself with their backgrounds.

There was a female employee who was a recovering

alcoholic. Reading the notes in her folder, Carole was pleased to see that the woman would soon celebrate her first year of sobriety. The bank had kept her on since she had agreed to attend the local A. A. meetings and visit with a counselor regularly.

The second file revealed an all-too-typical marriage mess. Carole recalled having tried to get the husband of this employee to listen to his wife's concerns. Now Carole wondered if they were still together. In any event it would take a great deal of tact and diplomacy to persuade the man to do his part to save the marriage.

The third case was the most interesting—a male employee who had been diagnosed as having multiple personality disorder. He was in several support groups, and was currently being treated by a therapist who specialized in these problems. Carole was to be his support link in his working environment, but it would be a challenge. She was never sure which of his personalities would be coming through the door.

So all-consuming was her involvement with the people whose lives she had shared so briefly that it seemed she had barely begun before it was five o'clock, time to quit for the day. Wrapping up the paperwork, she gave her secretary some instructions, then locked her office door behind her. Only then did Carole realize she was limp with exhaustion.

But she was also exhilarated. It had been a fulfilling day, one that had called for all the gifts God had given her...and then some. For a split second, she almost regretted having to leave the work until Wednesday. It would break her continuity.

On the way home, while she fought the five o'clock

traffic, Carole thought of the beloved husband and child waiting for her, and thanked God she had a family to come home to. She also took a minute to thank Him for Pearl's culinary skills and for the supper she would not have to cook!

The minute she hit the door, Carole kicked off her high heels, accepting with gratitude the frosty glass of iced tea Pearl offered her. After reporting that Tim had had a fairly calm day and was now sleeping, that Leigh was at Georgianna's house, and that Daniel should be reminded of a seven-thirty meeting when he came in, Pearl bustled off for home, as energetic as when she had arrived that morning.

"How does she do it?" Carole marveled under her breath, forcing herself from her chair to go check on Tim in the nursery.

Leaning over the crib, her heart skipped a beat at the soft perfection of her sleeping son. He stirred when she brushed a light kiss across the delicate skin of his temple, but he kept his eyes firmly shut. With a sudden rush of love, Carole realized how much she had missed him and longed to hold him in her arms. *Maybe by the time I've changed my clothes he'll be awake.*

She had just donned jeans and a shirt when she heard Daniel coming in the back door and rushed to meet him.

"How's the career woman today? Did everything go well. . .that is, after you finally got to work?"

His wide grin obviously meant he was pleased to see her, and she led him into the den, eager to share her day. "I lifted my head twice and the day was over."

He listened patiently to her recital, making an occasional comment, asking a question to clarify a detail, but otherwise not interrupting the nonstop flow of her tale.

"You were right, Daniel," concluded Carole, "my life *was* becoming too narrow. I had forgotten how thrilling it is to help people, have an impact on their lives—" She paused, watching his reaction. "But you must feel this way all the time."

He studied her flushed face with concern, then said quietly, "I just hope neither of us forgets our real priorities."

Tim was still asleep, so Carole went into the kitchen to check on the dinner Pearl had left in the oven. As she set the table, she found herself replaying the events of the day. One case, in particular, had touched her, and she toyed with the idea of asking Daniel for his opinion, then dismissed the thought. It was her first big case on the new job, and she wanted to wrestle with it on her own.

Hearing Tim's cry, she started for the nursery, only to meet Daniel in the hall, with his son in his arms. "Look who's up."

Carole hurried over to take the baby from him. "Hello, my sweet. Did you miss your mother today?"

Walking back to the kitchen, she cuddled him, inhaling the sweet baby smell, and felt a small pang of guilt as she realized she had barely had time to give him a thought all day.

Daniel followed them, helping Carole put Tim in his little swing. When he asked about Leigh, Carole told him, "She's eating at Georgianna's."

"Again? Maybe they should take out adoption papers on her."

Carole chuckled and they sat down to eat.

But Tim was not happy in his swing. "What's the matter, little one?" Carole asked, taking one last bite and lifting the baby from the canvas sling. "Mommy's here now, and I'll be with you all day tomorrow. We'll do some catching up then."

Usually the sound of her voice soothed him, but tonight nothing she did seemed to please him.

"Pearl said he's teething. Maybe that's what all the fuss is about," suggested Daniel.

Using a clean diaper, Carole ran it around his tiny gums. "Daniel, I do feel a sharp little point here in the front!" Tim seemed easier as she massaged his lower gums. "His first tooth. Our baby's growing up."

Daniel gave a wry smile. She was like a little girl with her first big doll. "I think that's what they're supposed to do, isn't it?'

"Is teething supposed to make them so irritable?" she asked, concerned. "I'm going to get out my baby book and see if there's something I should be doing for him."

She handed Tim over to his father and went to the den library. Returning with the book, she found what she was looking for. "Hmmm, here it is. Something cold. Teething ring filled with water in the freezer. Frozen juice. Well, that's easy enough. And according to this pediatrician, Tim is a little ahead of schedule, too." She closed the volume with a sigh of relief and looked up just in time to catch Daniel's smug smile. "What are you grinning about?"

"You. Heaven help us all if Tim doesn't develop on that doctor's schedule."

Feeling a little foolish, Carole gave him an annoyed glance. "I know I worry too much sometimes. But I find it very comforting to have an expert on call. I've never had a baby before, you know, so I don't know when to call a doctor and when to let nature take its course." She laid the volume down on the kitchen counter and took the baby from him. "Besides, just think of all the money we'll save if I don't run to the doctor every time he sneezes." She heard Daniel's sigh, and wondered if he were wishing he got that kind of attention, too.

He had a distant look in his eye as he gathered some papers and crammed them in his briefcase. "I have a meeting to attend. You and Tim play Eskimo. I'm sure he'll be fine."

Carole was disturbed by the expression on her husband's face. It was a lonely look, and it tore at her heart. "I'll wait up for you," she promised.

Hope leaped into Daniel's eyes. "Then I'll make it a quick meeting." His step was light as he hurried out the door.

But when Daniel returned, the scene wasn't what he had hoped to find.

Carole, looking more frazzled than before, was in the nursery, holding Tim. "This teething must be a bigger deal than I thought. He's still very uncomfortable, no matter what I do for him."

"Let me try. You go take a hot bath." Daniel took Tim and sat with him in the rocker while Carole headed for the bathroom.

"Son, we've got to have a little talk," Daniel began,

speaking softly to the child. "I know you love your mother and need her. But I'll tell you a little secret. I need her, too. I want you to be an especially good boy tonight and go to sleep. You may have to tough out this teething thing, but I know you can do it." As he talked, the baby grew drowsy. "That's a good boy," he said as he eased the child into his crib and slipped out of the room.

Carole was already in bed, wearing a beautiful lacy gown, her auburn hair fanned out on the pillow. And she was sound asleep.

Quickly Daniel got ready for bed and climbed in beside her, making as much noise as possible. She didn't move. He thumped and plumped his pillow loudly and bounced around a bit as though to get comfortable. She didn't stir. Longingly he looked at his beautiful wife lying beside him, so deeply asleep he feared she'd miss the last trumpet call. He leaned over with one last attempt. *It worked for Prince Charming,* he thought as he kissed her on the lips. But it didn't work for him.

He rolled over to his place and bent to the inevitable. He knew it had been a hard day for her at the bank. He also knew she had put in the equivalent of another day's work taking care of Tim. In his heart, he understood all these things, but his disappointment wouldn't be denied.

And just as quickly, disappointment turned to anger. He felt unloved, uncared for. Fear rippled through him when he remembered the last time he had felt this way. Susan Lapney had tried to fill that void!

His heart beat faster, and he immediately began to pray, *Lord, give me patience with Carole and her new job. Help me put my life into perspective. And please, God, don't let*

Susan Lapney do anything to hurt me or my family or my ministry. Protect us all from this woman.

In spite of his prayers, Daniel didn't fall asleep right away. He wondered what Carole would do if she learned that Susan thought she was in love with him. Would Carole love him more? Would she be more attentive to his needs? He shuddered to think what could happen, and fell asleep at last, with more prayers that Carole wouldn't have to find out.

thirteen

Daniel awoke feeling exhausted, even before his day got underway. He knew Carole had gotten up with Tim several times during the night, but he had made no attempt to help her. *She can sneak in a nap sometime during the day,* he thought, not feeling very charitable toward her after last night's letdown.

He slid out of bed, careful not to wake her. A steaming hot shower put some zip back into his step. Then he went to the kitchen for his coffee. With Carole still sleeping, though, he had to settle for cold cereal for breakfast. Wistfully he envisioned homemade pancakes with hot butter and syrup sliding off the stacks. He was feeling terribly sorry for himself. It was safer than feeling angry at Carole.

On the way to the office, Daniel mentally reviewed his plans for the day. Heaven only knew, however, what the actual day would bring forth. One day in the life of a busy pastor was never like the one before.

Rhoda was already at work when he arrived. He always looked forward to seeing her cheerful face.

"Good morning, Boss. How's the newest member of the working wives' club?" She handed him a cup of coffee and led the way into his office.

"I think it will all work out eventually," he said, as much to convince himself as to answer her question. "Yesterday was a little harrowing. Tim is teething, and Carole's day

128

was the usual stressed-out first day on the job. But I keep reminding myself, what kind of damage could three days a week do us?"

Rhoda laughed. "That's what my husband said when I came to work here at the church." She smoothed her cream-colored skirt down around her legs and gracefully crossed them.

It had long been their habit to begin their workday with prayer, a cup of coffee, and some small talk, giving the two an opportunity to gear up for the day before tackling the important business of the church.

But today Daniel's question couldn't wait, and he plunged in as soon as they were seated. "Rhoda, was it much of an adjustment when you started to work, even part time?"

"Not at first. Of course, I had no children, so I didn't have as many obligations as you and Carole." She took a sip of her coffee. "But after a while, a very short while, as I recall, it did get to be a bit much. In my time, men were not expected to do any of the housework. And my little job was considered almost a hobby. But when things did finally get to the boiling point, my husband, bless his soul, jumped right in and did what he could to help." Her eyes behind the large glasses, misted slightly. "He was the kindest man I ever knew. A lot of fun, too. I suspect it was his sense of humor that was the secret of our long and happy marriage."

"I wish I had known him," Daniel said quietly.

She regarded him fondly. "In many ways you could have been his son, Daniel. You have so many of his qualities." With a faraway look in her eyes, she rose and walked toward the door. "Maybe that's why I sometimes treat you as I would a son of my own."

"I'm afraid you're not quite old enough to be my mother, Rhoda, but I do accept the compliment."

"Just follow my husband's example, and keep a sense of humor about this big new thing in your life. I suppose you're still wrestling with your call, too? In time God will tell you what to do," she assured him, "about both of them." Then suddenly she was all brisk efficiency once more. "And now, you'd better get to work. You have a counseling session at ten o'clock."

"Yes, ma'am," he called to her retreating back. Mumbling to himself, he added, "And people have the silly notion that I run things around here."

Scanning the appointment book Rhoda had left with him, Daniel saw that in addition to the morning counseling session, she had kept his afternoon free for hospital calls. At least two of his shut-ins would be counting on a visit. Tuesday was also the day for planning presentations for any meetings he would be conducting during the week. At the council meeting this evening, for example, committee members would be expecting some kind of report on his recent visit to Stephenville, and perhaps even a decision on whether or not he would be taking the call.

The call. What should he do about that? Daniel reached into his desk drawer and pulled out a folder containing the notes he had made while visiting St. Paul's. Rereading them now, he updated them, adding new information that had come to his attention since the trip. He had hoped the trip to Stephenville would give him a clear-cut picture of things. *But the decision is getting harder,* he thought. *Now there are also Carole's job and Leigh's college plans to consider. What should I do now, Lord?*

Before he could receive any insights, the phone buzzed. That phone call required two more to settle the problem before he was free to concentrate on his report once again.

Finally he was able to draft an outline that satisfied him. He would tell the committee that he hadn't made up his mind, but make it clear that the call to Stephenville was still a viable option for him. He also knew it wouldn't be fair to keep either congregation in suspense for too long, and felt the pressure to arrive at a decision soon.

He filed his report just as Rhoda ushered in his first appointment—a young couple who had come for counseling.

It was a stormy session, and part of the time Daniel felt more like a referee than a counselor. But they were able to make some headway in the discussion of their problems and agreed to come the following Tuesday for another meeting.

Daniel finished up some paperwork, then decided it was time to clear the air with Carole. He wasn't mad anymore. But when she picked up the phone, he was careful to keep his voice casual. "How are things going today with Tim's teething?"

Carole sounded tired and cross. "Terrible! This is supposed to be my day off, and all I can see are all the things I didn't get to do yesterday." He was beginning to regret having called home when she added, "I'm sorry, Daniel. About everything. I didn't know I was so tired. And then Tim cried all night long, and he's cried all day today. I hate to say it, but I'm almost glad I have to go to work tomorrow. I don't think I could stand his fussing much longer."

"Call the doctor and see if he has anything that will help.

Surely there's something he can do."

"I already have a call in to him, so I'd better hang up in case he's trying to reach me with a miracle cure." Her voice softened as she said, "I love you. . .and I'll see you tonight." There was a long pause. "And, Daniel, I promise to be more cheerful when you come home. If the doctor sends something out soon, I'll try to get a quick nap in . . . you know, so I won't fall asleep on you again," she said in a sheepish voice.

Daniel couldn't help laughing. "It's a deal. But tell me, how is it you can always seem to read my mind?"

"I'm a woman," she replied simply. "Why? Does it make you nervous?"

"No, but I think I'll be more careful in the future about what I fantasize around you."

"And with *whom*," she added mischievously.

The scene with Susan Lapney flashed through his mind at the sharp reminder, and Daniel made a sudden decision never to mention that episode to Carole. No harm had been done really. Besides, he was trying to forget it himself. They hung up and he hurried to the hospital, willing himself to put the whole thing behind him.

Daniel's first visit was to a parishioner who was dying of cancer. The man was still in the denial stages of his disease, and Daniel prayed mightily that he would have tact and sensitivity in dealing with this person who would meet his Maker within a few short weeks.

The wife, meek and mousy-looking, skittered around the bed, waiting on her husband hand and foot. Daniel wondered how she would take his death when the time came. He had the feeling it would be a devastating blow, since she was obviously very dependent on her husband for everything.

The next call was a cheerful one. Visiting with a new mother was always a joy, but even more so since Tim's birth, he decided. After a prayer for the new life and a promise to be available to the parents whenever called upon, Daniel left for home, eager to be with his own little family.

The sun was still clinging tenaciously to the horizon when he rolled into the drive. *Maybe it's cool enough for supper on the patio. I could put something on the grill and give Carole a break,* he thought with a surge of compassion.

All was quiet when he entered the house. He didn't call out, thinking with a smile how well-trained he had become. Carole was asleep on the couch in the den, and a hasty peek in the nursery revealed that Tim was snoozing in his crib.

Poking his head into Leigh's room, he found her cleaning out her closet.

She looked up at his soft greeting. "Hi, Dad. Have a good day?"

"Yes, as a matter of fact, I did. You look busy. What are you doing?" The room was littered with clothing, stacked in piles—on the floor, on the bed, thrown over a chair.

"Classes will be starting pretty soon, and Carole told me to go through everything and see what I'll be needing." She wrinkled her nose distastefully. "Some of these things have to go."

"Do you know if the doctor called?"

"He called, and the pharmacy sent something to help Tim sleep."

"Well, I have a meeting tonight and Carole's asleep. Why don't you and I whip up a quick supper and surprise her?"

Daniel could see Leigh's hesitation. But she didn't put up an argument, and followed him into the kitchen.

Quickly they fired up the grill, put on hamburgers, and set out the trimmings. "Thanks, champ." Daniel leaned over and kissed his daughter on the top of the head.

Then he went into the den and knelt beside his sleeping wife. "Wake up, Sleeping Beauty. Time to get up and greet your loving husband." He nuzzled the warm spot between her chin and shoulder.

She stirred lazily. "Hmm. What's that lovely smell?"

"My aftershave, I guess."

"No, I mean food. Did Leigh cook supper?" She moved to get up from the couch.

He felt a little crestfallen but resisted the temptation to take the credit. "Let's just say Leigh and I collaborated on it. Come on, everything's ready."

Carole checked on Tim first and was visibly relieved when she came back from the nursery, pronouncing him down for the night after the strong medicine the doctor had prescribed.

Table talk was of clothes and school and friends. Leigh told a funny tale about an escapade she and Georgianna had experienced recently. Carole spoke of her new job and her concern over Tim's illness. Daniel listened in silence, waiting for an opening in the conversation. It never came.

At bedtime, when Carole slid in beside him, Daniel longed to reach for her, but felt constrained. Why didn't he feel he had that right? He waited for some kind of signal, some interest on her part, but there was nothing. He knew she was juggling some heavy responsibilities right now, and he wanted to be considerate of her needs. But why couldn't he just reach for her and enfold her in his arms as he wanted to do? Had she forgotten what she had promised him? Had she changed her mind?

I'm not going to let this opportunity pass, he thought doggedly. *Tim is asleep. Carole had a nap. She promised me that tonight—* He moved over and took her in his arms. And though she did not resist his kiss, he felt no real response from her.

Carole's mind was still churning with Tim's discomfort, planning what course of action to take with her clients, what to wear, wondering if she had put out the menu for tomorrow for Pearl. She knew what Daniel had in mind. But she couldn't focus on lovemaking right now. Still, she had promised—

She tried to concentrate, tried to feel romantic. It was pleasant to feel him so close, kissing her, loving her, but she felt no real passion. She simply gave herself up to him, letting him hold her.

Daniel knew things were different tonight. Carole was compliant, but certainly not enthusiastic. What was wrong? He lay still, his arms still wrapped around her. "Where are you tonight?" he asked softly.

"I'm right here."

"But not really."

She looked into his dark brown eyes. "I love you, Daniel, and it's enough tonight for me to give you my love ... quietly." She kissed him again to reassure him. "The passion will come again when I'm not so. . .splintered. Please bear with me. I need time."

"I know that's what you keep saying. It's what everyone keeps saying." He sighed. "OK. Time. You've got it," he said without rancor. But in his heart, he knew it would be a very long while before he approached her again.

Daniel tried to make himself comfortable for sleep, but felt he had barely drifted off when he was disturbed out of his light slumber.

"Daniel, wake up!" Carole's voice was tense with worry. "I can't do a thing with Tim. He's been crying for an hour. What should I do?"

"Maybe we'd better call the doctor," was the brilliant solution concocted by his sleep-sodden brain.

Hearing his son's shrill cries, Daniel stumbled out of bed and took the little boy in his arms while Carole dialed Ethan Stewart's number. After the brief conversation, she swung into action. "He said meet him at his office."

They threw on some clothes, bundled up Tim, and headed for professional help.

Ethan was waiting for them when they arrived at his office. He examined the screaming baby calmly and diagnosed the problem almost immediately. "He has an ear infection. Hold on, little fellow," he soothed the child. "It'll be all better in a short while."

He administered a shot while Daniel turned his head, unable to bear the sight of the needle penetrating the soft flesh. "He'll be fine now. I've given him a shot of antibiotics and enough painkiller to get him through the night." He scribbled out a prescription on a pad and handed it to Carole. "Get this filled in the morning and follow the directions carefully. He'll be tip-top in no time."

Daniel had always felt a warm affection for the bearded young professional, and now he felt a great respect for his ability as well.

Ethan's white teeth gleamed through the rust-colored beard. "This is the first time he's been sick since that scare in the hospital, isn't it?" He patted Carole on the shoulder. "You're doing fine, Mom. You did all the right things. And never hesitate to call me when things like this happen. I got my degree at night school," he quipped.

Carole laughed. "You're a wonderful doctor, but a terrible comedian."

"Our best to Beth, Ethan." Daniel shook his hand gratefully. "And thanks again."

"Don't mention it. I'll do that when I send you the bill."

"With a generous professional discount, no doubt," Daniel shot back.

"OK, you two," Carole interrupted. "Let's get Tim home. Tomorrow is a workday for me." The baby was already settling down sleepily in her arms.

On the way home, she had another problem on her mind. "What should I do about going to work tomorrow? I hate to think of leaving a sick baby with Pearl."

Inwardly Daniel flinched. *Here we go.* "Well, since you're just getting started, maybe it wouldn't be a good idea to miss work," he admitted reluctantly. "Would you feel better if I worked out of the house tomorrow instead of the office?"

"Oh, Daniel, would you?"

The look of profound relief she gave him was almost embarrassing, especially in view of his ungracious feelings.

"You've had so much more experience with a sick child

than I have. And Pearl could come in and do the housework." Her face glowed in the illumination of the street lights. "I love you," she said softly. "Thanks for being so wonderful."

Daniel only sighed. Another crisis resolved. What could possibly happen next?

fourteen

It wasn't such a bad day.

Tim was a little cross, occasionally rubbing his ear with a tiny fist, but after Carole left for work, he accepted Daniel's care without complaint. It was Pearl who seemed a little miffed when she learned she had not been left in charge of the sick child. Still, she commented that she was glad to see Daniel taking fatherhood so seriously.

Bless Pearl's heart, she did everything she could to make the day run smoothly for him. It was almost like having Carole at home again, and Daniel began to enjoy the unorthodox experience.

So this is what it's like to manage a household, he mused as he drank a cup of hot coffee, thoughtfully provided by Pearl, and caught up on some reading, in between phone calls from Rhoda, who was working at the office.

Many of his parishioners were more than a little astonished to find their pastor at home, caring for the sick baby. There was even a little admiration for his gesture, and he began to feel somewhat heroic. When one woman told him she couldn't imagine her husband staying at home with their kids, Daniel made an attempt to play down the uniqueness of the situation, being careful to let her know how upset Carole had been in having to leave Tim.

He was not surprised when Tillie called. And it was to her he stated his case most plainly, for Tillie would be the official spokesperson for this landmark event in his life.

The phone rang again. "You really are one in a millon. No wonder I love you so!"

Hearing Susan Lapney's voice, praising him for his noble sacrifice, Daniel's composure exploded into a million pieces. "Susan," he said firmly, "I thought we had this all settled." He listened for sounds in the house that would tell him where Pearl was currently working. "We agreed you shouldn't call me like this."

Even the sternness in his tone did nothing to diminish the warmth in hers. "I know, but this couldn't wait." Petulantly she added, "Don't worry, I won't call you again. Not unless it's really important, that is. As long as I can see you at church, I'm happy." When Daniel didn't respond, she added, "What have you decided about your call to that other church? You aren't going to leave, are you? I just couldn't stand that."

"Susan, God has chosen me to do a very important job for Him. If anyone were to find out how you feel about me, it could cause all sorts of problems." He did his best to convey the message kindly, but with great authority.

She was instantly contrite. "I'm sorry. I won't call anymore, I promise. And I won't tell anyone, either. It will be *our* secret. But don't ask me to stop loving you. It's the only thing that keeps me going."

He thought he heard an underlying threat and it alarmed him. "I'm counting on your promise, Susan. If you really do love me, then you would never do anything to harm my family or jeopardize my work. Isn't that right?"

"Yes." Suddenly her tone took on an air of formality. "Of course, Pastor. I know exactly what you mean. I'll certainly do the best I can. Thank you for calling. Goodbye."

Daniel's hand was shaking as he replaced the receiver. Obviously someone, probably her husband, had come in. *That crazy woman called me while her husband was there! Or else he came into the room unexpectedly.* Beads of perspiration popped out on Daniel's forehead. *I'm in over my head.*

Taking a deep breath, he reached for the phone, then paused, listening. He couldn't afford to be overheard now. He rose and closed the bedroom door.

"I'd like to talk to Dr. Stewart, please," he told the receptionist. It was only seconds before Ethan came on the line.

"Tim's fine," Daniel assured him before rushing on. "It's something else, a professional matter. I have a major problem, but I don't want to discuss it over the phone. Could we meet sometime soon?"

"Tomorrow's my day off. My office or yours?"

"Why don't we take a short drive into the country? Maybe to Lake O'the Pines?"

"Fine. Ten o'clock?"

"Ethan, this may take awhile."

"Whatever it is, we can at least get a handle on it. Ten o'clock sharp."

If there was anyone in the world Daniel trusted, both personally and professionally, it was Ethan Stewart. Ethan had a degree in Christian counseling as well as a medical degree. He had been more than helpful in the past. Now Daniel desperately needed his advice, input, support. But what he needed most was someone he could confide in.

"Thank You, Lord, for a man I can trust." Daniel rotated his shoulders and rubbed the back of his neck. "Please help me with this problem. Show me what to do and say to help this woman. Send Your Spirit to guide and sustain me. And, Lord, protect my family—"

He had barely finished his prayer before the phone rang once more. It was Rhoda. "Mr. Smith just passed away. His daughter called and says her mother needs you. Can you go?"

"I'm on my way."

Daniel shook off his own troublesome thoughts and left for the hospital, ready to pick up the burden of the grieving family. *Even now, Lord, in the midst of the biggest crisis of my ministry, You remind me that someone else is suffering more than I.*

On the drive to Lake O'the Pines next morning, Ethan asked no questions, but treated the entire matter routinely, as if this were standard procedure for busy doctors on their only day off.

Spending the first few minutes catching up on family news, Daniel put off telling Ethan the reason for his call. Finally, he launched into a recital of everything that had happened. The obvious attempt at seduction, running into Susan everywhere he went, and last of all, her call to his house.

"I'm a little afraid of her, Ethan," Daniel concluded. "I don't know if she'll keep all this to herself or not. And I can't think of a way out of this mess."

Ethan had listened carefully, nodding from time to time. Now he came right to the point. "I should think you *would* be. She could be dangerous. Not physically, of course, but she could certainly damage your reputation if this ever got out." Not waiting for Daniel's reply, he hastened to offer consolation. "But, pal, you wouldn't be the first professional to be tarred and feathered."

Daniel pushed back against the seat, watching the pine trees flash past, the heat shimmering off the hot asphalt. "I'm really in that much trouble, huh?"

"You could be." The teasing tone was noticeably absent. "If she should tell anyone her version of what happened that morning at her house, you could be in a lot more than just trouble. No witnesses, just the two of you. Could be messy."

"I really appreciate your cheering me up like this," Daniel managed with some sarcasm. "I feel so much better." He turned into the picnic area beside the lake and switched off the engine. "Any ideas?"

"The obvious one is to get her into therapy, but that seems like a long shot right now." Ethan turned in his seat to regard Daniel. "Does Carole know anything about this?"

"Of course not." At the disapproval registering in Ethan's expression, Daniel added, "I *couldn't* tell her. The episode shook me up, and I wasn't ready to deal with it." The excuse sounded lame, even to him. "Ethan, we're in such a state of transition with the baby, the job, and Leigh, I didn't want to add anything else. At the time it seemed better to forget it. And I thought I had made my position very clear to Susan." He rubbed his hand over his face and rolled down the window to allow the cool lake-fed breezes to blow through.

"She isn't going to let that stop her, you know." Ethan rolled down his window, too. The picnic area was sparsely populated, and there was certainly no danger of anyone hearing their conversation. "Susan is no different from any other woman who falls in love with a professional man. We're in a position of authority. We're morally clean, they think. The very fact that we are 'ideal' makes us vulnerable. In that woman's eyes you're everything her husband isn't. You're a servant of the Lord. Loving you makes her feel closer to Him. And if she can get you to make love to her, that will be her ultimate gift to God, her ultimate communication with Him."

Daniel shivered. "Stop it, Ethan! That's blasphemy!"

"Not in her mind. We're dealing with fantasy, not fact. I hate to tell you this, but I don't think you've seen the end of Susan Lapney. And you'd better find a way to deal with it before it blows sky high."

"But what?" Daniel could almost anticipate what Ethan would say, but he waited for his friend to tell him what he already knew.

"Call her into your office. Confront her with the fact that you know she's having marital problems. Offer *my* services." He grinned crookedly. "That is, if you think I can help her."

"And if she doesn't agree, what then?"

"I'm afraid you don't have many options left. What would happen if you went to her husband?"

"Don't even think about it. Ethan, I'd feel like a fool."

"Then let's try Plan A."

Daniel ran his hands through his dark hair and propped his chin on his elbow, resting it on the window ledge of the car. "She seems like such a nice woman. How did all this happen? How did she get so messed up?"

"Right now I don't have a clue. But if I can find out, we'll have something to work with. It's not uncommon."

"Maybe not. But it's never happened to me before." Daniel paused, pondering the dilemma. "And you definitely think I should tell Carole." It wasn't a question, it was a commitment.

"As soon as possible. Just in case anything happens." Ethan was uncharacteristically serious. "Make sure everyone, I repeat *everyone* knows how much you love your wife. If you two are having problems, patch them as quickly as possible. Show affection in public. And in private, smother her."

Daniel couldn't help laughing. "I'm sorry, but if you only knew how much I want to do that. But with the baby and her job, well let's just say I haven't been able to do as much. . . smothering. . . as I think I have a right to do."

"Right? That's an interesting way of phrasing it. Are you feeling left out, Daniel? That, too, is a common problem."

Quickly Daniel responded, "Now, don't start on me. I came out here to talk about Susan." He opened the car door and swung out his long legs. "Why don't we walk under the cool pines for a while?"

"Running, Daniel?" asked Ethan innocently.

"A little, counselor, but I'm learning to cope with my feelings." With great earnestness Daniel added, "I've gone through a period of significant change in my attitude about marriage, and other things." He turned to face his friend. "It's been a long hard road, but I think we're finally over the hump."

Ethan slapped him on the back. "Attaboy! Hang in there. I've had a few adjustments to make myself." Daniel thought of Beth, the widow with two children, whom Ethan had married within the past year.

"Life is rich and full," Ethan went on. "Once in a while we hit a snag, but nothing stays the same forever. That's the most important thing I've ever learned." He smiled broadly through his rusty beard. "Nope. Nothing stays the same forever."

Carole could hear Leigh playing with Tim in the den as she dressed for the Smith funeral the next morning. Today was theoretically her day off, and she was glad she was free to be at the church with Daniel and the bereaved family. She adjusted the top of her royal blue coat dress with the big white collar. A respectful color, but not one of deep mourning.

She could imagine how the widow must be feeling right now, since the pain of Samuel's death had not entirely been erased by her love for Daniel. But she knew she had grown from her experience and could deal compassionately with the survivors.

"We won't be gone for more than a few hours, Leigh," Carole said as she reached for her car keys. "If you need anything, we'll be at the church or the Smith home."

"Tim and I will be fine. Don't worry about us." Leigh smiled appreciatively at her stepmother. "You look nice."

Carole hurried over to drop a warm hug around her shoulders. "Thank you, my sweet. See you soon."

Life with Leigh was presently tranquil, Carole thought gratefully. Her stepdaughter even seemed more accepting of suggestions she had made lately. *And having Tim didn't hurt my stock with her, either,* she mused.

Carole entered the quiet sanctuary and found her usual pew halfway down. The heavy sweet smell of flowers brought back memories of long ago. Still she didn't feel sad today.

When at last the widow and immediate family were

seated, the service began. Daniel's sermon on the resurrection of Jesus and its meaning for this day blessed Carole, and she basked in the sure knowledge that she and her own family, as believers, would one day be with the Lord.

After the brief committal service at the cemetery, she spoke with the dazed widow, then found Daniel.

"Going over with me to the house for the meal?" he asked.

"Yes, Leigh is with Tim." Carole felt her husband's strong hand on her arm, guiding her to the car, and was grateful that he was still with her—vitally alive and well.

But she was frowning as she slid into the front seat of the car. "I guess Joyce is mad at me. Probably because I haven't seen her in ages. I haven't even had time to call her," she admitted ruefully.

"What makes you think she's mad?"

"She deliberately avoided me at the service and again at the committal. I can't blame her. I haven't been much of a friend." It grieved her that she had so little time for Joyce. But life was so full now.

Inside the Smith house, some of the ladies were setting out a generous buffet. Tillie headed up the committee with her usual gusto and smiled when she saw Carole and offered her a plate.

As she filled it, she looked around. Through the kitchen door, Carole spotted Susan Lapney, hard at work. She looked very attractive today in a light summer dress. *What a worker that woman is! She's at the church everytime they unlock the doors,* a painful reminder that Carole herself wasn't. *Ancient history,* she thought. Nowadays there was never time to do all the things that were expected of her.

After the meal, Carole watched as Daniel leaned down to comfort the silently grieving widow, whispering some final words of consolation for her ears alone, and giving her a warm hug.

Those are the arms that hold me, Carole thought, hugging the idea to her. She knew the strength his arms could impart and felt a deep sense of God's extra blessings that she should be the one—the only one—to whom Daniel turned for his own consolation and comfort. *I really must be more available to him.*

As they drove home, she sat close, savoring his nearness.

Daniel broke the silence. "Carole—" he began, deep in his own roiling thoughts. "I think I need to make one more trip to Stephenville to speak with the council. I keep feeling a tug I can't account for." He gave a shuddering sigh. *If she only knew everything that's bothering me these days.*

She glanced at him anxiously. "Am I making it hard on you? My job, that is?"

"Partly," he confessed. "But I still believe there is a lot I can accomplish in this parish. It's just that I can't get a clear reading on the Lord's plan in all this."

They pulled into their drive and sat talking for a while.

"When will you leave and how long do you plan to be gone?"

"Oh, only overnight. I thought I'd fly down Monday and be back Tuesday morning." He was silent while both of them mulled over the problem. "What do *you* think I ought to do?"

She struggled to be impartial. "The easiest thing would

be to stay here—" She tried to imagine the enormous change in their lives if they were to move to Stephenville, and gave up. It was too frightening—"but if you go down there and you're absolutely positive you should go, call me. You know my heart is here in Longview," she said truthfully. "I think I'd be happy if we could stay here forever."

He sighed deeply. "Maybe we should put out a fleece like Gideon did when he needed a sure sign from the Lord."

Carole knew he wasn't joking. Many times in the past, she had asked the Lord for specific guidance, expecting Him to answer so clearly there could be no misunderstanding as to what He wanted her to do. And He had answered her. Some might put it down to coincidence, she knew, but she was convinced that if she listened hard enough, she could hear Him say yes or no or wait awhile.

Whatever the answer to this question, she did not doubt God's love for them. And He would tell them what they needed to know. . .in His own time.

fifteen

The phone was ringing as Carole entered the front door and tossed her keys on the gilded French marble-topped table in the hall. She didn't even have time to take off her shoes. How many times Daniel had teased her about her love of bare feet in the house.

She heard Leigh answer, then call for her. "Carole? Is that you? Phone."

"Yes, this is Carole Thornton," she said into the receiver, a bit breathless from hurrying.

"Carole, this is Susan Lapney. Is it true Pastor is flying down to Stephenville again?" She sounded very agitated.

"Yes, as a matter of fact, I just took him to the airport."

"I guess this means he's taking that call," she said dejectedly.

"No," Carole disputed her. "It means he's meeting again with the council to talk with them about it." She was irritated with the woman's bluntness, so she spoke with deliberate courtesy.

"But he *is* still thinking about it."

"Susan, you know that any pastor must seriously consider all the calls he gets."

"But this is the first time Daniel. . .uh, Pastor has ever gone somewhere twice."

The nerve of this woman! "I really can't discuss this with you right now, Susan. I just got home and I need to take care of Tim. Perhaps we can talk again later. Thanks for calling." She hung up before Susan could say anything more. *Who does she think she is?* Carole fumed.

When the phone rang again later in the evening, Carole almost expected it to be Susan, or maybe Daniel, saying he had reached Stephenville safely. But it was Tillie.

Carole was immediately on her guard. She could see Tillie's antennae quivering for information.

"I heard Pastor's gone to Stephenville again." Tillie fired her opening volley with no tact or preliminary amenities.

"Yes, he has, Tillie," Carole replied sweetly. She really did like the old busybody, but knowing the woman was the world's best and most active gossip, Carole was not about to give her anything to send over her hot line.

"Does that mean he's taking the call there?"

"No," Carole said for the second time that day, "it means he has gone to talk with the council again."

"He's still considering it, then," persisted Tillie.

Carole wanted to shout, "This is a recording!" but she took pains to answer politely. Before Tillie could get in the next question, however, she cut her off. "I'm waiting for Daniel to call me to say he's arrived safely, Tillie. I'll talk with you later. It surely was nice of you to be so concerned. I'll be sure to mention it to him when he calls tonight. 'Bye."

As soon as the line had cleared, Carole took the phone off the hook. Daniel had said he would not call her until after he had met with the council, maybe as late as midnight. She sighed as she explained the situation to a disgruntled Leigh.

"But, Carole, I promised to call Georgianna." Her face was set in a serious pout that promised some stormy hours.

Life with Leigh was very uneven at times. She seemed happy at home for the most part. But when the two of them were at cross purposes, Carole felt she didn't have the tools to resolve their differences. If she backed down, she might lose her status as a parent. But if she stood her ground, Leigh would shut her out for hours, or even days at a time.

Carole grasped at a quick solution. "All right, go ahead and call Georgianna, but if another call beeps in, you must promise me not to take it. I can't deal with one more person grilling me about Daniel's trip."

"I promise, Carole. I won't take any calls. Thanks, Mom."

In a daze Carole heard the unfamiliar term and smiled an enormous smile. *Maybe compromise is the name of the game with teenagers,* she thought, and made a mental note to find a good book on living with this new species of human beings so foreign to her.

She was feeling very warm and maternal as she bathed the baby and got him ready for bed. Tim cooed during his last bottle, keeping his big eyes fastened on her face. It was hard to give him up to the crib, but she tucked him in for the night, breathing a prayer for his protection. *Being a mother is a good job,* she thought happily. *I think I can recommend it.*

Quickly showering, Carole slipped into a gown and robe and tried to read a book on being a working mother. Unfortunately she found nothing on living with teenagers, and her mind strayed often to Daniel and the meeting he was attending. When she caught herself reading the same page over and over, she gave up.

Prowling the house to make sure everything was securely locked, Carole looked in on Tim and found Leigh also asleep, the phone by her bed firmly in the cradle.

She was barely back into her own bed for some more reading when the phone rang loudly in the stillness. "Hello?" It had to be Daniel.

"Carole, my darling, I miss you. I'm sitting here in a twin to the room we had in the Spanish Motel. Remember? And where are you, my sweet? A million miles away. What am I doing here?" He sounded euphoric, so different from his mood when he left.

"Daniel, are you all right? You sound so strange."

"Carole, you're not going to believe this, but something has happened I would never have expected. I mean I believe in it, of course, but I never thought it would happen to me. You know?"

"No, I don't know. Daniel what are you talking about?"

"I had an early dinner with John and Bethany Hallman, then went to the meeting," he explained. "And right there, during the devotion at the beginning of the meeting, it hit me—" He paused, searching for words. "I know this must sound crazy to you, but suddenly I knew, I just *knew* I should be at home. I could see the challenges of *this* church all laid out in front of me here, and it all looked so tempting. They even offered to raise my starting salary. I listened to everything that was said, and the feeling just kept growing. I knew I could do the job they were offering. I even *wanted* to do that job. But by the end of the meeting, I knew I should stay in Longview."

"Yes!"

"I explained as best I could what was happening," he went on, "and concluded by telling them I couldn't take the call at this time. Maybe sometime down the road, but not now."

Even over the phone, she could almost see his smile of relief. "I'm so happy for you, Daniel. The Lord has answered both our prayers."

"And what was your prayer, my love?"

"Only that you would find a definite answer one way or the other on this trip. But, Daniel, I'm as happy as you are. I really didn't want to move."

"I know. But you would have gone with me and been happy, wouldn't you?" he said with confidence.

"I told you I would *go* with you," she hedged. "*Happy* would have had to come later."

His chuckle came from deep down. "I love you, my darling wife, and I'll see you tomorrow afternoon when you get home from work. Good night, love."

"Good night, Daniel." She replaced the receiver and lay back against the pillows. "Thank You, God. Thank You, God. Thank You," she whispered to the starry sky that lay wide and blinking outside her bedroom window.

At work the next day, Carole said nothing about Daniel's decision. It was his announcement to make and she would wait for him. She had said nothing to Leigh, lest she make an innocent slip, and nothing to Pearl, who appeared a bit strained as she began her daily chores. She longed to wrap her arms around the older woman and tell her the good news, but held onto the secret for Daniel's telling.

When Carole returned at five, she almost sprinted into the house to greet him. She knew by the smile on Pearl's face that she had been entrusted with the big news.

Daniel kissed his wife unabashedly, right in front of Pearl, and hugged her mightily. "Tonight we celebrate. Pearl, you must stay and eat with us."

"Oh, no, Pastor," she protested. "This is a *family* celebration."

"Which is exactly why I asked you to stay. You are part of the family. I thought we had settled that at Tim's baptismal dinner."

Mist formed in the woman's faded eyes. "Then sit down and I'll put the food on the table."

The festive meal was not half over when the phone rang.

"I'll get it," Daniel said.

His voice on the phone in the den dropped, moving from gracious to grim, and Carole couldn't tell from his responses exactly what had brought about the change.

When he returned to the table, he looked strangely drawn, yet angry at the same time. "I have to go out tonight." He seemed to want to say something else, but held back.

"What is it? Has there been another death?" Carole felt fear claw at her stomach.

"No, nothing like that. I had hoped. . .that is, I'd wanted to tell you—" He sat down heavily. "I meant to tell you before—" He looked helplessly at Pearl.

"I think I'd better go," the housekeeper said hurriedly.

"No, I want you to stay. You need to hear this." He stood, pushing his chair under the table. "You finish your dinner. I want to talk to Carole first."

Carole followed him back to the bedroom, her stomach churning. Something awful was happening. What could it be?

Daniel closed the door and motioned to her to sit down on the bed next to him. He took her hand gently, as if to cushion the blow that would come with his words.

He began at the beginning, leaving nothing out. He told

her about his visit to Susan's house, the clothes she had worn that day, how frightened he had been when her behavior became seductive, how unbelieving when she said she loved him. He told of the times he had deliberately avoided Susan at meetings, never allowing himself to be alone with her again, and of his meeting with Ethan earlier in the week.

"We agreed she was unstable, maybe even dangerous, but the trip to Stephenville came up, and I haven't had time to confront her yet." There was a very long pause while he tried to collect himself. "Tonight she tried to kill herself."

Carole gasped.

"When her husband, Al, found her, he called the EMS. They pumped her stomach, and when she came to, she told her husband she was having an affair with me, that she was afraid I was leaving, so there was nothing left to live for. Al called George Williams, and George called me." Daniel ran his fingers distractedly through his hair. "I need to talk to Al and decide what to do. I'm going to ask Ethan to join us. Thank God I talked to Ethan! At least I have a witness to back up my part of the story." He heaved a body-racking sigh and looked at her sadly.

Carole was sitting rock still. She felt as if all those stars in the vast heavens she had prayed into last night had suddenly fallen in on her. Her mind was reeling, yet the words he had spoken were crystal-clear. Someone was in love with her husband. Someone had tried to take him away from her. Not just anyone, Susan Lapney. Pretty Susan, who was always there when the church doors opened. Susan, who had called her and then taken the pills after Carole hung up on her.

She sat in stunned silence. *Am I to blame?* she wondered. She thought of all the time and attention she had lavished on Tim, putting Daniel second in her thoughts for the first time since their marriage. Had Susan sensed his loneliness and moved in, hoping to catch him in a weak moment? Anger, fear, and guilt rocketed through Carole's body, leaving her with no air to breathe. She felt faint.

But when she looked into the face of her husband, she knew that Susan Lapney was nothing to him but a large problem. Her heart told her that Daniel loved only her, and he was waiting for her to say something, *needed* to hear from her.

"My poor darling." She wrapped herself around him, pulling him hard against her and cradling him like a child. She felt something warm fall on her face and heard the soft sound of his crying.

"I love you, Carole. She has never been anything to me. It's you I love with all my heart. Never have I betrayed you."

"Hush, darling," she soothed him. "I know that. I'm so sorry for all the times I've let you down since Tim was born. Oh, dear God, I am so sorry."

They sat on the bed, rocking and holding on to one another, saying over and over the words "I love you" until their misery was spent.

Daniel pulled back from her and reached for his handkerchief, wiping his eyes and then tenderly sopping at hers.

"Do you want me to come with you to the meeting?"

"No. I need to meet with George and Ethan first by myself. We must figure out what to do." He regarded her solemnly. "Carole, if people believe her, she could ruin me, ruin my ministry."

Never had she seen such sorrow in his eyes. "We'll fight her, Daniel. She can't prove any of the things she claims. Who's going to believe her?"

His smile was tired. "Anyone who loves a scandalous story. I can see the headlines in the paper now: 'Pastor Has Affair with Parishioner. Husband Punches Out Pastor Over Wife's Affair.' I could even be sued for malpractice. Can you believe it? I could be sued!"

She sat stupefied, disbelieving.

"After the meeting, I'll call the president of the district and tell him what's going on. I'll need all the help and advice I can get."

"What can I do?"

"Pray, Carole. Pray as you've never prayed before in all your life," he said grimly. "I need to go. Will you tell Pearl and Leigh what's going on? Tell them only the basic facts. I only want them to know that I am accused but I'm not guilty. Tell them—" His eyes began to fill again with unshed tears—"tell them that I love my wife more than any woman has ever been loved and I would never do anything to hurt her."

He kissed her and was gone, hurrying to the most important meeting of his life.

sixteen

There was a soft knock on the open door and Pearl and Leigh entered. Pearl was carrying a glass of water and a lace-edged handkerchief. She offered both to Carole.

"The hanky was my mother's," Pearl said. "I never go anywhere without a clean one." She took the space Daniel had just vacated, while Leigh, her eyes like a frightened fawn, sat at Carole's feet. "Can you tell us what happened?"

Slowly and painfully Carole told them the facts as Daniel had instructed.

Pearl's face turned white, and then red with anger. "Why that, that, oh, being a good Christian woman, I can't say what I want to! How dare she make up a story like that! She's sick, I tell you, sick!" She paced the room in anger. "Well, I can tell you this. No one is going to believe this ugly lie. No one who knows Daniel Thornton is going to believe these ravings. Oh, my dear, what a horrible thing for the two of you to have to endure. The devil is laughing in hell for sure tonight." She sat back down beside Carole. "I want to stay with you until he comes home. But what do you want me to do? Should I call someone?"

"No. Stay with me, please, and pray. We have to pray." She felt Leigh's hand grasp hers in silence. "There is no power on earth strong enough to handle this. Pray with me."

There in the semi-darkness the three women prayed,

each in her own fashion, beseeching God to take control. They begged Him for exoneration for Daniel, for the support of the congregation, and for Susan Lapney to come to her senses and deny this terrible lie. They prayed for wisdom and patience. Finally, when they had exhausted all the prayers they could think of, they sat quietly side by side.

When Tim began to fuss, Leigh slipped out to calm him.

"You know, when you first married Daniel, I was so angry," Pearl confessed. "I just knew that someone as pretty as you couldn't possibly be good for him. You wouldn't know how to take good care of him. I used to bake cakes so I could come and check up on how you were treating him."

Carole smiled in spite of herself. "I know. It used to frighten me terribly when I saw you headed up the walk with one of those cakes."

Pearl laughed out loud. "You knew! Well, all those tacky things I thought about you have come back to haunt me." Carole laid her head against the woman's shoulder, and Pearl wrapped her arms around her, like a mother. "I love him like my own, you know. And I have thanked God a thousand times that he found you. I've never known him to be so happy. Oh, not that he's perfect. Lord knows, I've fussed at him enough myself. He's messy, too."

Carole chuckled. "He told me he liked to spread the newspaper around the chair just to watch your eyebrows go up."

"That scamp! I should have known." Her delight faded as she spoke again. "Carole, I want to tell you I have prayed for forgiveness for all the ugly things I thought about you. Now I'm asking for *your* forgiveness."

Carole choked back a lump in her throat. "I'm sorry for all the things I thought about you, too." She looked miserable. "I dumped your cake down the sink once."

Pearl's laughter filled the room. "You're a winner, Carole. A real winner. And we'll win this fight, too. Just you wait and see." She softly whispered, "Thank You, Lord, for my family. I ask you to hold them in Your hand and protect them from Satan and all his devils. He's trying to ruin one of Your best warriors against sin. Don't let the devil win this one, Lord."

Carole began to cry, each tear a prayer that the Lord would take care of them.

It was close to one o'clock before they heard Daniel's car finally pull into the driveway. He looked exhausted when he came into the den and fell heavily into his favorite chair. The three of them sat on the couch, waiting anxiously for a report.

"It looks bad," he said. "I know George believes me, but this thing is going to hurt the church. God only knows the ultimate cost."

"Maybe He will use this to pull us together and make us stronger," Pearl offered hopefully.

"I pray you're right. But right now it looks as if the story is all over town. And it's gotten a little bigger each time it's told. I'll call the president tomorrow, and George is going to get in touch with Solomon Lake."

At the mention of the lawyer's name, Carole nodded in agreement. "I think that's a good idea. Surely Solomon will know how to handle this. You've done everything you can tonight, Daniel. Why don't we go to bed? Pearl, you sleep in Leigh's twin bed. It's too late for you to be out.

I'll get you a nightgown."

Obediently Pearl followed her and took the gown she offered. "I've never slept in anything this fine before. Thank you." She gave Carole a timid kiss on the cheek.

In their own bedroom, Carole dropped her clothes where she took them off, put on her gown, and climbed into bed beside Daniel. He was close to sleep as she kissed him good night. They wrapped their arms around each other. There seemed to be nothing more to do but hope that in the morning they would learn it had all been a very bad dream.

When Carole awoke, her benumbed brain attempted to register the day. *Wednesday, my day off,* she decided. But before she could enjoy that thought, last night's stunning turn of events bowled her over again, sending a shiver of premonition through her body.

Daniel was still sleeping soundly, his head pushed down hard into his pillow, almost as though he were fighting it. She slipped out of bed and put on her robe, careful not to wake him.

In the kitchen Pearl, already dressed for the day, was pouring herself a cup of coffee.

"You're up early this morning," Carole greeted her.

"I don't need much sleep anymore. It's either the blessing or the curse of getting older," Pearl commented wryly.

They sat companionably at the table, sharing the stillness of the morning and their coffee. The silence between them was not so much strained as thoughtful.

The phone shrilled at them, disturbing their reverie. "I'll get it," Pearl announced firmly. "Tillie," she mouthed. "Just a minute and I'll see if she's awake yet." She looked questioningly at Carole.

Steeling herself, Carole reached for the receiver. "Hello."

Anger cascaded across the line like a burst of fireworks. "I want to know what Pastor is going to do about that lying Susan Lapney!" Tillie demanded. Before Carole could answer, she raced on. "Anyone in their right mind can plainly see that he's crazy about you. Why, that mousy little twit can't hold a candle to you. I want something done about this today. The woman must be totally insane, that's all I can figure."

Tears threatened to spill over onto the phone as Carole tried to find her voice. "Thank you, Tillie," was all she could manage.

"Only thing in the paper this morning was that she tried to kill herself. No names or anything. Foolish woman." The derision in her voice softened to a gentleness Carole had never heard before. "I just called to let you know that you and Pastor have my complete support. Mr. Wilcott's, too, of course." The gruffness came back. "We'll fight this thing to the last ditch. No one is going to lie about our pastor and get away with it. You stay strong now." And she was off the line.

Carole stood holding the dead receiver for a few seconds, trying to regain her composure. Then she lay the phone down on the counter. "I just can't take any more kindness today."

Pearl put the phone back on the hook. "I'll handle it. People need to be able to talk to someone. They'll understand if they can't speak to you or Pastor." She smiled knowingly. "I can be very uninformative when I want to be, but I won't hurt their feelings."

Carole took a cup of coffee to the bedroom to awaken Daniel for the meeting he was to attend this morning. They were tender with one another, careful not to jar the delicate balance between them.

When he left, Carole had an encouraging word for him. "Things are going to work out," but she wasn't sure she knew just what she was promising him.

All three women spent the morning in a daze, their hands automatically busy about chores, while their minds were on the meeting Daniel was now attending. The house had an eerie quietness without the ringing of the phone, for it had sounded off not once more. Leigh's animated chatter was missing. And only baby Tim grinned, totally oblivious to the seriousness of the struggle in which his father was engaged.

Carole felt herself in a state of constant unspoken prayer, reaching for God with her very being. The words in the book of Romans floated through her mind: "Likewise the Spirit helps us in our weakness; for we do not know how to pray as we ought, but the Spirit himself intercedes for us with sighs too deep for words."

She clung to this promise to keep her from drowning in fright.

It was getting close to noon when Daniel came in. He looked strained. "Its going to be bad," he said stonily. "No matter how it's handled, this is going to be bad." He sat down in his chair as if his knees would no longer support him. "Solomon said there are several things we can do. We could sue for libel, but that would drag things out over a long period of time and give the news media a field day. And he feels it wouldn't serve the purpose of getting Susan to retract her statement and get some help for herself." He sighed. "Solomon has arranged a meeting with Susan's husband and Ethan. Surely Ethan can convince him that Susan is lying and needs professional care." His eyes held a dim hope.

"And then?" Carol was almost afraid to ask.

"And then a church council meeting. Ultimately Solomon feels we'll have to have a congregational meeting to totally clear the air."

The four of them sat without comment, trying to comprehend the magnitude of the problem before them.

"Solomon is meeting right now with the editor of the paper. With Ethan's professional opinion for support, he feels he may be able to get the story played down."

"We have a good editor," Carole reminded him, "not one who puts out yellow journalism. Surely he'll help." At least she wanted to believe this with all her heart.

"Anyone call today?"

"Tillie. I hope Susan stays out of her way. Tillie's liable to wring her neck like an old hen for the soup pot."

"I gather she's on our side." The corners of Daniel's mouth turned up the slightest bit. "Anyone else?"

"No."

He looked startled. "No one? I need some feedback, even if it's bad. I wonder why no one else has called."

They looked helplessly at one another. Why, indeed?

"When will the meeting with Susan's husband take place?" Carole asked, to break the silence.

"Solomon was hoping for tomorrow. I'll know tonight."

In the silence that followed, each person in the room tried to assimilate the news and make it manageable. Carole felt fear quake through her, alternating with numbness. All the prayers she wanted to say distilled down into only one phrase: *Help, God, help.* Mostly she felt herself reaching out to Him wordlessly, with the helpless gesture of a pleading child.

The hours dragged by, and when the phone finally did begin to ring, Carole flinched. There weren't many callers, but without exception these few were outraged at the ugly rumor and wanted Daniel to know it. But why hadn't more people tried to get in touch with them? Was it possible most of them believed the worst about their pastor?

When Solomon called in the early evening, the news was hopeful. Carole heard Daniel agree that tonight would be fine for their meeting.

"Al will meet with us at eight." Daniel's jaw tensed and released as he flexed it in anxiety.

Carole walked to him and wrapped her arms around his waist wordlessly. Everything she thought of to tell him sounded like a cliché, so she offered her love and support silently.

The light supper Pearl prepared went largely uneaten, and then it was time for Daniel to go.

"I'm praying for you with all my heart," Carole whispered as he bent to kiss her goodbye.

Daniel sighed, squared his shoulders, and said with strained cheerfulness, "I know." And then he hurried out the door.

Carole wondered if this was what it was like to send a man off to war. It was a war for them, wasn't it, and who knew how long it might last, or its consequences?

The phone didn't ring once during the maddeningly slow evening.

When Carole mentioned that fact to Pearl, the woman

remarked, "Let's count it as a good sign."

By the time Daniel returned home, Carole was actually trembling with the tension pounding her body. But she didn't miss the tired upward turn of his mouth.

"Well?" she demanded. "How did it go?"

"Al believes me. It took a lot of explaining and talking, but I think he knew from the start that his wife needs help. He just didn't know how badly." Daniel moved to the kitchen with the trio following close behind, opening the refrigerator for a soft drink.

"What happens now?" Pearl asked. She didn't look as relieved as Carole felt.

Al believed Daniel! That should clear up everything.

"He has agreed, very reluctantly, I might add, to appear before the council and refute Susan's story. He's not eager to face this thing publicly." Daniel's eyebrows crunched over his dark eyes. "I just hope he doesn't back out on me."

"You don't really think he'll change his mind . . . or his story . . . do you?" Carole asked.

He regarded her steadily. "I can't be sure of anything at this point." He drank deeply from the cold can and sat down at the table with its stubbornly cheerful yellow cloth, while the women settled around him like a flock of birds. "Did I have any calls?"

"Not even one," Leigh replied.

He shrugged. "I wonder if that's good or bad."

"We voted it was good," Pearl declared.

"Daniel—" Carole moved closer, looking up with her chin at its familiar jut. "I want to attend the council meeting. I am on the council, you may remember." When he didn't answer immediately, she added, "The meetings are no longer private, and I want us to be seen as a united couple."

His large arms reached for her, enfolding her, accepting her request with his embrace.

"We're a team," she went on. "I need to be there with you. It will make a strong statement to the people." Her eyes glittered with mock mischief. "And I promise, I won't say a word."

"No matter what?" he prodded her.

"No matter what," she agreed. "Unless someone asks me a question, of course."

"Carole," he warned, then saw the laughing tilt of her brow. He caressed her tousled head. "It may get bloody."

"I've been bloodied before."

"Not like this." Glancing around, Daniel saw that he and Carole were alone in the kitchen. Pearl and Leigh had made a discreet exit. He used up another of the seemingly endless sighs that stretched before him. "I've never had to defend my personal integrity before."

"It's your word against hers," Carole said. "Certainly she can't provide any witnesses. The only proof is in her fantasy."

"I do have Ethan. I've thanked God a thousand times for that."

"Don't forget God and me." The look was not sanctimonious, just a friendly reminder.

"How could I forget, my darling." He looked at the table, fingering the weave of the cloth. "Please don't misunderstand me, Carole. I know I'm innocent. But I've lived long enough to know the `good guys' don't always win. Sometimes things happen for which we have no earthly explanation."

"Like our losing Ellen and Samuel," she said softly.

"Yes." He took her hand, resting on the tabletop, and held it, running his fingers lightly over hers.

"But then we found each other." She knew he was hoping they could come out of this thing unscathed. "What will we have lost this time, I wonder?" Her eyes begged for one small hope.

"Some things that are irreplaceable, and irrevocable." He used up another sigh. "My skeptical side says my ministry is tarnished forever in this town . . . maybe even more widely . . . even if I'm proven innocent. And we both know how hard innocence is to prove."

"And your optimistic side?"

"It says something good will eventually come from all this. It has done one thing already." He tilted her chin with his hand so that she was looking into his eyes, and willed her to believe him more deeply and surely than ever before. "My first thought was that you'd believe Susan, and I'd lose you. Never have I ever loved you more than now. I'm ashamed to admit that I was cross, no, mad, at you for the time you spent with Tim. I felt even less important when you started to work." A deep flush of embarrassment stained his neck, and spread over his face. "But I know I love you, and I'm learning to share you."

She sprang from her chair, knelt before him, pressing her face against his broad chest and wrapping her arms around his waist. "My own true love. I knew how you felt about the baby. I'm so sorry I didn't do a better job of taking care of you both. I felt so torn." She wanted to prove her love to him. "I'll quit my job, if you want. It's not that important."

He was deeply touched. "No, I couldn't ask you to do that." There was a split-second pause. "Besides, we may need the money." The implication was obvious.

"Always with the jokes," she complained.

"Who's joking?" he said grimly. "I've never thought about the possibility of losing a church." She could see the silent shudder running through him. "The disgrace of it all would be almost impossible to live with, I would think."

She wanted to comfort him, but anything she could think of to say would sound hollow, even to her own ears. And the reality of it all was too stark to ignore.

"I'm exhausted. Let's go to bed." He rose and walked slowly down the hall toward their bedroom, moving as though he had aged a thousand years.

seventeen

Carole was aware of Daniel's tossing and turning throughout the night. She slept almost as poorly as he, and they both rose the next morning, foggy with fatigue.

The silent telephone became a sinister symbol of isolation. There was neither support nor condemnation coming over its serpentine line. Carole had never been so aware of the instrument before, and she wanted it to ring, needed to hear a warm voice on the other end.

Pearl came in, even though it was not her usual day, and began her chores with determined cheerfulness.

Daniel and Carole got ready for the day, moving slowly and thoughtfully. With Leigh and baby Tim still sleeping, their breakfast together was uninterrupted, but strained. It was as if they were both holding their breath, waiting for something to happen.

When he was ready to leave for the office, Daniel kissed Carole goodbye, promising to be back for lunch.

Carole spent her morning caring for Tim and finding ways to keep busy. She could hear Pearl humming in the kitchen, and the sound had a soothing effect on her.

At noon, Daniel came in for lunch, looking a bit happier.

"Good morning?" Carole asked as she served him.

"Not bad. I had a few calls. Positive one. Rhoda is fit to be tied. I'm not going to give her any more letters to type today. She nearly beat that poor computer to death this morning." He grinned, pleased at the overt expression of support.

Carole felt herself responding to his lighter mood, and they shared a pleasant meal, laughing at Tim's antics as Carole fed him.

Daniel hadn't been back at work but a few minutes when the phone finally broke its silent ban. Carole took a deep breath and answered it, mentally preparing herself for anything.

She wasn't ready for this, though.

"Carole." It was Daniel. "Stephenville has sent me another call."

Carole knew that occasionally a church sent a second call to a prospective minister, but this was the first time it had ever happened to her husband. "What!"

There was a pleased timbre in his voice. "Yup. They met and voted to call me a second time. What do you think?'

"I think I'm stunned. What do you think?"

"I'm wondering if the Lord is trying to tell me something. I really struggled with that call the first time. St. Paul's had so much to offer. Now, I'm not sure how it will look if I take it."

"You think people will think you are running."

"Yes," he replied simply, then added, "I'll have to completely clear my name before I leave this place, even if it takes years."

"Daniel, be reasonable. You can't stay in a place just to prove something to people. That's not what a call is for. You're back to square one again, but you don't have to decide anything today."

"I know. But I can't help thinking that if things don't

work out here, the Lord has given me a place where I can go and lick my wounds." He sounded so resigned.

"Daniel Thornton, you make me mad! Don't you dare talk like that! Giving up before the fight has even started." Her face reddened with anger. "Has the meeting been scheduled yet?"

"Yes. George called to let me know it is set for tomorrow night. Al said again he will be there. Ethan, too." She could hear the strain in his voice. "I wish it were over."

"Me, too," she agreed softly. "But not until after we've won."

This time there was a note of reverence in Daniel's tone. "It never fails to amaze me how mysteriously the Lord works. I'll bring all the information home tonight. Maybe there's somethinhg new in there I've overlooked. . . .And thanks for the verbal spanking, darling. I'm having a hard time sorting things out right now. And you have such a tactful way of bringing me back to earth."

After supper they sat at the table and reviewed all the information about St. Paul's again. There was one interesting item. The salary had again been raised. Modestly. But definitely raised.

As they sat there surrounded by papers, Carole had the feeling she was watching a movie, with someone who looked exactly like her playing out her part in the drama. Her husband's calling as a minister was on the line, his reputation in jeopardy. He once again had a call that could very well catapult them into a new life in a new place. It was too much to cope with at one time. She shook her head to clear her thoughts.

They talked and speculated, Daniel doing most of the weighing of information while she listened . . . and prayed.

"There is one more thing to consider." Daniel's face was sad. "Will they still want me when they hear of the mess I'm in?"

The thought hadn't crossed her mind. "I—I don't know."

He got up from the table and put out his hand to pull her up with him. "Let's let the Lord take care of it. It's too big for me."

Settled in the safe haven of their bedroom, Daniel's affectionate good-night turned warmer. Carole felt herself reaching for him, needing confirmation of their love. Daniel responded in kind, each of them giving totally of themselves.

She whispered, "Don't ever let me go."

"Not a chance." He stroked her face gently with a trailing finger, looking into her eyes. She could see the reflection of her own love there in those dark brown ones.

"If only the doubters knew how much we love each other, they would laugh Susan out of town," she said.

"I just can't imagine my life without you, Carole." His eyebrows knotted over his searching eyes. "And there is no way I can ever tell you how important it was for me that *you* never doubted my fidelity."

"The thought did flash through my mind," she confessed. "But I know you so well. I knew there wasn't another woman in your life. You have your hands full with *me*."

They slept, knowing only that their love was secure.

The next morning was spent in a running conversation

with God, Carole alternately pleading with the Lord for His mercy and reminding Him of all the promises He had made to those who love Him. There was not a moment of the day that passed without the memory of His past mercies and guidance, and she reminded Him of that fact. She reminded Him of Jesus' death and resurrection for them and the forgiveness of all their sins. She recounted passage after passage that promised God's love and action in His people's lives.

Her prayers were not frantic ones. Actually, she was rather surprised at herself. She was relatively calm, considering what was at stake. When she thought it all out, she knew she was not afraid of the outcome as much as what might be said at the meeting.

"I thought I had learned how to handle criticism," she mumbled to herself, "but I don't know if I can stand to hear anyone say anything against Daniel."

He didn't come home for lunch, choosing to spend that time with Ethan and George, preparing for the meeting. Carole couldn't eat a thing, but fed Tim his lunch and put him down for a nap, watching him sleep for long moments. Every breath was a prayer.

Carole dressed carefully for the meeting, but casually, in a softly printed summer dress and her favorite low-heeled sandals. As she was pulling her hair back from her face and securing it with a golden clip, Leigh came in.

"You look wonderful, Mom." Her face plainly showed her loving concern.

"Thank you, honey. Sure you don't mind staying with Tim?"

"Absolutely. Don't give us a thought." She picked up

Carole's ornate perfume bottle, tracing the gold filigree with a careful finger. "I want Dad to know I've been praying very hard about tonight. I'm positive God won't let anything bad happen."

Carole pulled her close. "I don't think He will either." She sat back down at her dressing table and ran the brush through her hair one last time. She could see Leigh's reflection in her mirror. How much she loved this dear young woman. How much joy Leigh had brought to her life. Carole was well aware that a time of crisis could either divide or unite a family.

Daniel came in from Tim's room. His face was drawn and his jaw clenched. "Ready to go?"

"Yes." Silently she kissed Leigh on the cheek and followed her tall husband down the long hallway.

Neither of them spoke during the short drive up the winding road to the church's meeting hall. Carole felt her nervous stomach tighten with a lurch at the sight of the cars parked around the building with its lighted windows. It didn't look like the warm place she remembered.

Daniel's on trial tonight, she thought. *We're both on trial. What if the church council doesn't believe him? No, don't think about that!* she cried inwardly. *They must believe him.*

She reached for his hand and gave it one last squeeze before they left the car. They walked to the door, Daniel's arm protectively around her shoulders as if to shield her.

Inside, the tables had been set up to form a large U, with George Williams sitting in the center of the middle table. Some of the people looked up as they entered. On the lookout for friendly faces, Carole was rewarded with a few welcoming smiles.

But it was the eyes that were averted or covert that alarmed her. The air was crackling with tension. It reminded her of the last act of a murder mystery, just when the villain was about to be unmasked. Who would be the villain tonight?

Al Lapney was there, wound tight and ready to bolt.

Ethan came to meet them and offered chairs next to his.

Then Pearl joined them, giving Carole's arm a friendly squeeze. Rhoda sat directly across from them, her face set in a mask of defense.

Joyce was sitting nearby and hurried over to give Carole a big hug that re-sealed their friendship without words.

There were murmured hellos and quick, warm handshakes, but Carole also noted some impassive faces. Waiting faces.

For one awful moment, Carole thought she would laugh out loud, for there at the next table sat Hazel Platther, knitting a sweater. Was she also knitting all the names of the people involved in this "trial," as had Madam La Farge in *A Tale of Two Cities*? It was too ghastly to be funny, yet in her nervousness, Carole had to squelch her hilarity.

Good old Tillie was there, too. Her sharp eyes flashed a friendly greeting from across the room, her too-red lipstick painting a smile on her hawk-like face. Whatever happened here tonight would be fully revealed tomorrow over the telephone, good or bad.

George called the meeting to order and asked Daniel to open the meeting with prayer.

"Lord God, we are gathered here to deal with some very serious business. We ask that You be present. Help us to listen carefully, weighing all things by Your loving scales. Let our words be kind and constructive. Let us do nothing to dishonor Your Son's name in whom we pray, Amen."

Carole felt the tears form behind her closed lids, adding her own silent prayer to Daniel's. *Please, God.*

George cleared his throat. "As Pastor said, we have a very serious matter to discuss tonight, and I'll be following parliamentary procedure carefully. Please do not speak unless you are recognized. We all want to hear everything, I'm sure." There were a few muffled laughs, then silence.

"It has been brought to the attention of the council that some charges have been brought against our pastor. Specifically, the charge of leading an ungodly life, namely, committing the sin of adultery.

"Following the examples set down in Matthew, we have visited with Pastor and given him the opportunity to speak to these charges. We have also visited with Susan Lapney. She didn't dispute the charges. Following that, we talked with Al Lapney, who claims to have no knowledge of the alleged affair. Dr. Ethan Stewart was also present in a professional capacity. So I'd like to turn the meeting over to Dr. Stewart now for his assessment of the problem. Ethan?"

"Thank you, George." Ethan's gaze swept the group, focusing on individuals as he spoke, bringing a feeling of intimacy to the gathering. "I'm pleased to have this opportunity to share some very important information with you. I have spoken with Susan Lapney and her husband Al. And though the details of that conversation are confidential, I can tell you several things that have a direct bearing on the charges brought against our pastor."

There was not a sound in the room as Ethan continued. "Being a professional, particularly one in the public eye, carries with it the element of risk, but none so grave as the one we must address tonight. After spending some time with Al and Susan Lapney, it is my professional opinion that Susan has a deep-seated mental problem. Not an unusual one, but one that has serious repercussions for innocent people."

Carole was relieved to hear this subtle reference to Daniel's innocence.

"Without boring you with technical jargon," Ethan went on, "I feel Susan is living in a fantasy world, and in that world she has chosen Daniel as the hero. To her, he is the closest thing to God she can find, and needing this, she has built a world of dreams in which she plays a primary role in his life. She will need time in which to heal, and proper care before she will be able to function in an adult world. Her husband has agreed to help in every way possible, but until she can live in the real world, we must consider the things she has told us as wishful thinking."

He looked around the circle of faces again, strengthening his eye contact. "I see no need to take any kind of action against the object of her fantasies, but rather deal with her problems. A fine man's reputation has been severely damaged. It is the responsibility of this group to circle the wagons around him and stamp out the temptation to make something out of all this. As Christians, we must do nothing to shame our Lord, our church, or the man who so faithfully serves it."

Carole's gaze darted around the table, attempting to read the response to Ethan's plea. She saw heads shaking in a positive manner. Others were still sitting quietly, weighing Ethan's words. And there were others with doubt written all over their faces, like dirty fingerprints on a white wall.

"The chair will now open the floor for discussion and questions."

An expectant hush fell over the crowd. Carole held her breath. If it was to come, it would be now.

A hand went up. "I hate to be the one to ask the first question, but I think we owe it to ourselves to ask a few and give Pastor a chance to defend himself. I'm not disputing what Ethan says. I know it's certainly possible that what he says is true. I would like to know, though, if anyone has ever witnessed any improper behavior between Pastor and Susan. If so, they need to speak up."

Carole's heart thumped alarmingly in her chest as she saw another hand go up. What had he seen?

"I just want to say I've never seen Pastor treat her any different than he did the rest of the women." Several heads bobbed in agreement.

Al had sat quietly throughout the discussion. Finally he took a deep breath and raised his hand. "I'd just like to say that I'm afraid my wife has fabricated this whole deal. I know she has problems." He stared down at the carpet in embarrassment. "I should have done something about it before now, but it never got out of hand before." The misery he was feeling was plainly etched on his sun-browned face. "I'm just a working man. I do the best I can. Ethan has promised to help her get better. I'm sorry for all the trouble she's caused." His eyes pleaded for understanding.

Carole could feel the crowd's sympathy for the man and his wife. They, too, were embarrassed by the entire episode. How much worse it would have been if Susan had been there! Ethan's decision to let Al speak for her had been well founded.

She was also immensely relieved that this hearing was not being conducted as a trial, but a clearing of the air. The presentation of the facts would help everyone decide individually how best to handle the gossip.

Another hand shot up. Primly Mrs. Jones chirped, "I think I believe Ethan and Al. However, I do know that Paster called on Susan in her home on at least one occasion when Al wasn't home. 'Course he's made calls on a lot of us when husbands aren't around. But——" And here she intoned judgmentally, "it doesn't look too good to some folks,"

Rhoda nailed the offensive speaker with her eyes.

Daniel's face colored slightly, but he waited for any other comments before he spoke.

Then Pearl's hand went up. "You all know how I feel about Pastor and Carole. There isn't a finer family in the world. I see them on a daily basis, and I can assure you that Daniel Thornton is in love with his wife and would never ever do anything to hurt her. With all the love I see in that household, there couldn't be any room for anyone else in his life." Tears formed suspicious pools in the pale blue eyes. "I've never met a more honorable man."

If anyone had come to the meeting hoping to obtain some juicy tidbits to discuss over the telephone tomorrow, they were sorely disappointed. The atmosphere in the room was now one of friendly support and a distaste for what had to be done.

At last Daniel cleared his throat. All eyes fastened on him as he made his official statement. "I want to thank all of you for the kind words," he said humbly. "All my life all I've wanted was to serve God as a pastor. I worked hard to get my degree and have enjoyed every minute of my ministry." He paused and added, "Well, *almost* every minute." He waited for the soft laughter to die down. "I know about the things that can happen to a pastor. The pitfalls. I've known people who have been caught in those pitfalls, have had to pay a heavy price for their mistakes. I know that if I stay in my office and do my work, I will be criticized for not being out making calls, and if I go out and make calls, I will be charged with never being available when people need me.

"A person in the ministry must hear God's voice for himself, must follow God's priorities and not allow those to be foisted upon him by others. He must have a clear sense of his mission, and be willing to carry it out. Sometimes that gets a person in trouble with his parishioners. I know there is no way to please everyone, so I do the best I can. If someone calls and asks me to come, as Susan did that day, I don't ask myself how it will look to someone else, whether it is 'proper,' though I am not totally ignorant of propriety." His mood lightened. "I knew an older pastor who had a buzzer in his office, and after a female caller had stayed what he considered to be a proper length of time, he would push the button unobtrusively and his wife would come in carrying a tray of tea for three."

There was a burst of hearty laughter.

"As we all know, that won't work most of the time in today's society for many reasons. A minister must use his common sense to protect himself from compromising situations. On a few occasions, when there counseling sessions in the office, my dear secretary, Rhoda, has helped me avoid some unpleasantness. She has a good sense of when to buzz me and when not to. Thank you,

Rhoda."

Rhoda's mask crumbled with a teary smile and she nodded graciously.

"I will here publicly state that I have conducted myself with honor in every call I have ever made, either in my office or in a home. I love my wife more than I have words to tell you. I cherish the sanctity of our marriage vows and I have never ever violated them.

"There is no doubt that any professional, or anyone else, for that matter, has ample temptation put in the way now and again. Sometimes I'm flattered. That's the humanity in me. But I have never done anything of which I am ashamed. I will continue to weigh each situation on an individual basis and do my job as I see it."

There was a warm round of applause and enormous smiles as Daniel concluded. Carole could feel the tension in the room released in those clapping hands.

"Let me warn you that we can't dismiss all the gossip that will continue even after this meeting." Daniel studied each face. "People must talk this thing out. You will be accosted in the grocery stores, the gas stations, and at work. One firm statement from you can shut this thing down more quickly. If people see that you are not willing to speculate on my behavior, they won't try to keep the conversation going.

"Our church will take a beating over this for a while, but if we conduct ourselves as real members of the body of Christ, we can maintain our dignity and our credibility in the community. And let me add, that all of you have handled this matter with the utmost integrity. You came to me first. Gave me the chance to tell you the truth." A few heads ducked slightly away from his gaze. "Thank you for practicing what I preach."

Only Carole could know how much this meant to Daniel. It was a test of sorts, for all of them. Daniel had preached the Gospel to them, had been an example, and they had responded as Christians to a terrible dilemma. They had risen to the occasion. A church in a storm, and they all conducted themselves on the highest level. How proud she was of them!

But Daniel was not finished. "There is something else I need to share with the council." Muffled conversation gave way to respectful attention once more. "Stephenville has called me again. I received the official call document yesterday. Of course, I haven't had time to make any decision yet, but under the circumstances, it will be twice as hard. If I decide to take the call, it will not be based on anything that has happened here. I will pray and consider where I can best serve the Lord."

In the stunned silence that followed his announcement, Carole reached for Daniel's hand.

George rose slowly. "Pastor, first I want to thank you for your words of explanation about the Lapney matter. Second, I think I speak for all of us when I say we don't want you to go. I had hoped for some measure of respite after we dealt with, well, what we had to. It grieves me deeply to hear you are considering this call, and I personally hope you send it back tomorrow."

The group seconded his feelings with their applause.

"If there is no further discussion, I think I'll close this meeting. I'm bushed." He scanned the tables. "Meeting adjourned."

Daniel pushed himself upright as people crowded around him. Time after time Carole heard words of support and hope that he wouldn't take the call to Stephenville. They were not only for Daniel. She was warmly included.

When the back-patting and loving words were over and they were finally on their way home, all the pent-up tears raced a scalding trail down Carole's face.

"Tears now?" Daniel asked. "But it's all over."

"I know. That's why the tears. These are tears of relief, you dummy."

He pulled into the drive and parked, and pulled her into his arms. "It's all over now, my darling. The worst of it, anyway."

"Oh, Daniel, I just knew God wouldn't let us down. He couldn't."

"No, He can't," Daniel whispered softly, "even though sometimes it feels He's far away from us for a while." He caressed her hair gently, smoothing it from her forehead. "And, darling," he said quietly, "I'm going to return the call to Stephenville."

"Oh, yes, yes, yes!" cried Carole.

"In time the gossip will die. The people who count believe me. I won't be pushed out of the place God has put me." He grinned a crooked grin. "It isn't going to be easy. But when the soldiers opened the fiery furnace, Shadrach, Meshach, and Abednego were still there, unsinged. And Daniel was still in the lions' den, unharmed. We're going to stay in Longview," he said with finality, "and let God close the mouths of the lions."

Carole sighed. "I'm not sure I like the examples. Maybe," she said hopefully, "it won't be that bad."

Daniel chuckled. "When all this started, I expected to build larger spiritual muscles, but this has been like training for the Olympics."

Carole laughed softly, then grew silent. "Daniel, I think I've spent my whole life waiting for tomorrow to bring a better day. I should have been living each one of those days fully. After all, today is yesterday's tomorrow."

His smile was lazy, and his brows crinkled up with acknowledgment. "So where will you and I live from now on?"

She kissed his lips softly. "Today, my love, today."

A Letter To Our Readers

Dear Reader:

In order that we might better contribute to your reading enjoyment, we would appreciate your taking a few minutes to respond to the following questions. When completed, please return to the following:

Karen Carroll, Editor
Heartsong Presents
P.O. Box 719
Uhrichsville, Ohio 44683

1. Did you enjoy reading *Yesterday's Tomorrows*?
   ☐ Very much. I would like to see more books by this author!
   ☐ Moderately
   I would have enjoyed it more if _____

   _____

2. Are you a member of *Heartsong Presents*? Yes   No
   If no, where did you purchase this book? _____

   _____

3. What influenced your decision to purchase this book? (Circle those that apply.)

Cover	Back cover copy
Title	Friends
Publicity	Other _____

4. On a scale from 1 (poor) to 10 (superior), please rate the following elements.

    __Heroine   __Plot

    __Hero   __Inspirational theme

    __Setting   __Secondary characters

5. What settings would you like to see covered in *Heartsong Presents* books?

_____

_____

6. What are some inspirational themes you would like to see treated in future books?_____

_____

_____

7. Would you be interested in reading other *Heartsong Presents* titles?   Yes   No

8. Please circle your age range:

| Under 18 | 18-24 | 25-34 |
| 35-45 | 46-55 | Over 55 |

9. How many hours per week do you read? _____

Name _____

Occupation _____

Address _____

City _____ State _____ Zip _____

······ Heart♥ng ·····

Great Inspirational Romance at a Great Price!

Heartsong Presents books are inspirational romances in contemporary and historical settings, designed to give you an enjoyable, spirit-lifting reading experience. You can choose from 52 wonderfully written titles from some of today's best authors like Collen Reece, Jacquelyn Cook, Yvonne Lehman, and many others.

HEARTSONG PRESENTS TITLES AVAILABLE NOW:

(If ordering from this page, please remember to include it with the order form.)

·········Presents·········

ABOVE TITLES ARE $2.95 EACH

SEND TO: Heartsong Presents Reader's Service
P.O. Box 719, Uhrichsville, Ohio 44683

Please send me the items checked above. I am enclosing $ _____
(please add $1.00 to cover postage per order). Send check or
money order, no cash or C.O.D.s, please.
   To place a credit card order, call 1-800-847-8270.

NAME _____

ADDRESS _____

CITY/STATE _____ ZIP_____

LOVE A GREAT LOVE STORY?

Introducing Heartsong Presents —

Your Inspirational Book Club

Heartsong Presents Christian romance reader's service will provide you with four never before published romance titles every month! In fact, your books will be mailed to you at the same time advance copies are sent to book reviewers. You'll preview each of these new and unabridged books before they are released to the general public.

These books are filled with the kind of stories you have been longing for—stories of courtship, chivalry, honor, and virtue. Strong characters and riveting plot lines will make you want to read on and on. Romance is not dead, and each of these romantic tales will remind you that Christian faith is still the vital ingredient in an intimate relationship filled with true love and honest devotion.

Sign up today to receive your first set. Send no money now. We'll bill you only $9.97 post-paid with your shipment. Then every month you'll automatically receive the latest four "hot off the press" titles for the same low post-paid price of $9.97. That's a savings of 50% off the $4.95 cover price. When you consider the exaggerated shipping charges of other book clubs, your savings are even greater!

THERE IS NO RISK—you may cancel at any time without obligation. And if you aren't completely satisfied with any selection, return it for an immediate refund.

TO JOIN, just complete the coupon below, mail it today, and get ready for hours of wholesome entertainment.

Now you can curl up, relax, and enjoy some great reading full of the warmhearted spirit of romance.